PRAISE FOR STEVE L CLARK

"Clark takes the idea of the haunted house and flips it on its head in a masterful way. It's a story full of loss, grief, wonder, magic, and compelling lore. I was hooked from the first chapter to the last."

Brandon Applegate, *author of Those We Left Behind and Other Sacrifices*

~

"This is a book that will stick in your mind long after finishing it. Steve Clark crafts a riveting tale of horror that gives you goosebumps and pulls on your heart strings at the same time. If you're looking for a fresh take on a classic horror genre, look no further than The Doors of Chamberlain."

Matt Wildasin, *author of Melancholia, Baggage, and the Horrors Untold series*

~

"A perfect blend of reality and etherea[illegible] Chamberlain cranks up the suspense from page one and refuses to loosen its grip even after the story ends. Welcome to the new face of cosmic horror."

Chuck Buda, *author of Boondock Butcher*

"Absolutely riveting! I had to know what happened next and devoured it in one sitting. Horror has found a new home and it lurks behind The Doors of Chamberlain."

Grisly Details

THE DOORS OF CHAMBERLAIN

STEVE L CLARK

The Doors of Chamberlain
By Steve L Clark

Edited by Brandon Applegate

Cover art by Matt Wildasin

Interior Formatting by Brandon Applegate

ISBN 9781965316009

For my wife Jessie. The heart of this book is a love story, and I wouldn't know how to write that if not for you.

CONTENTS

PART ONE

I

Janie frowned at the overflowing post office box. The postmaster's voicemail stated she had three days to collect her mail or it would be removed. She had listened to it with the same disinterested gaze that had become her default appearance.

Her thin arms flexed as she pulled, twisted, and yanked, struggling to free the bundle of papers. Finally, they erupted and fluttered to the floor.

She squatted and scooped the stray letters into a pile, stacking them on top of a bulky brown envelope. The sunshine through the front window of the post office made her nearly luminescent. Her complexion had gone from moderately tan to a ghastly pale in the few months since Mark disappeared. The orange sun dress she wore hung loosely on her frame. Ribs showed through the oversized arm holes. She had always been thin, but now bore the jagged edges of malnutrition. Deep gray pockets under her eyes were the only spots of color remaining on her face.

With more effort than should have been necessary, she stood to her full height and exited the post office, passing the metal shutter pulled over the window on her way out. She was relieved no one else was in the office, sparing her any stares or attention. Haven Hills was a small town with an even smaller population. Everyone knew Janie Marris, and everyone knew Mark was gone. The local news reports of the Haven Hills man gone missing while filming a reality tv show were a hot discussion topic. They gave sympathetic condolences to Janie when they caught her out, and watched her descend through despair and grief as if it were a reality show of its own.

The crisp air of a fall morning greeted her as she descended the post office steps. Two teenage boys stepped aside as she passed them on the sidewalk.

"Faces of meth, bro," one of them said.

"Get that girl somethin' to eat," said the other.

It wasn't the first time she heard the joke. She was the poor girl who lost her fiancé and turned to drugs to cope. It wasn't true, but she didn't have the energy to argue. That, and she didn't care. It wasn't drugs rendering her into the wraithlike figure she had become. Grief consumed her, a piece of broken heart clutched in each gnarled hand.

She finished the two-block trek from the post office back to the house. Like her, the small house was neglected. The grass grew wild. Weeds sprouted in clumps and yellowed patches gave way to mounds of dirt pushed skyward by moles. The windows were streaked and grimy, highlighted by closed blinds Janie no longer opened. A garbage can overflowing with white trash bags sat at the edge of the house with more bags piled around it. Trash pickup was Friday mornings, but it had been weeks since Janie dragged the can to the end of the driveway. Her red Oldsmobile Alero sat parked in the same place it had been for two months. A squirrel watched intently from underneath the rear bumper as Janie crossed the driveway, climbed the two steps onto the small front porch, and let herself inside.

The gloom of the house was a welcome retreat from the caustic sunshine and prying eyes outside. She locked the door behind her, walked to the kitchen, and dropped the stack of envelopes onto the cluttered table.

She wanted to crawl back in bed and let sleep take her, but there were urgent matters to attend to. The stack of mail undoubtedly included bills with big, red FINAL NOTICE stamps plastered on them. Their meager savings were dwindling. With Mark gone, and Janie too distraught to return to work, there was no income. That the world would carry on business as usual, despite her world screeching to a halt, felt terribly unfair.

She grabbed an energy drink from the mostly barren refrigerator and resigned herself to deciding which bills to pay now and which ones to delay until the inevitable shut off. She sat in the rickety kitchen chair at the head of the table.

Several of the letters were pre-approved credit card offers. She gave them all a cursory glance before tossing them to the side. Next came the electric bill that now featured a payment plan option to avoid disconnection. She breathed a sigh of relief, though she knew it would only grant her a temporary reprieve. Better than having to come up with the full balance now. The water and cable bills followed. She tossed the cable bill onto the credit card offers. Let them shut it off. She hadn't watched television in weeks.

The last item remaining was the brown packing envelope. There was no return address, only her name and address written in black sharpie in big letters across the front. She tore open the package. A flash drive clattered onto the table. Janie's brow creased as she pulled a single piece of paper from the envelope. She read the three sentences scrawled on the paper and then read them again, her hand trembling.

Mark is not dead. Watch the videos. I need your help.

2

For a moment, she considered snatching up the flash drive and throwing it in the trash. It was a cruel joke. It had to be. She thought of the kids taunting her on the sidewalk. There were people out there who said nasty things—did nasty things to torment others.

It made no sense. Why now, after all this time? Mark would have come back if he were alive. He would never have left her alone. No, she thought, if he was alive, she would know. He had to be dead. The thought of him in the world without her while she wasted away in isolation and despair was too much to process.

She picked up the flash drive and rolled it around in her fingers. For such a small piece of plastic, it carried substantial weight. Whatever was on the drive would change things. If there was nothing, or worse, a mean spirited joke at her expense, she would have to accept the world had taken a further step towards labeling her an attraction to be mocked. If Mark was on the drive, if there was anything to suggest he was still alive, everything would change.

She closed her eyes, said a silent prayer, and carried the drive to the living room. Her laptop sat open on the coffee table. She tapped the power button, but the screen remained dark. Groaning, she pulled open the drawer under the table and grabbed the charger. A wad of tangled cords snaked out of the drawer with it, and she fought to untie the knots.

"Come on, fucker!" Her initial misgivings were replaced by an adrenaline she hadn't felt since those first few days after Mark went missing. She felt a flicker of life.

The cord came loose from the knot. She dropped the tangled mess back into the drawer, thrust the charger block into the wall, and the cord into the side of the laptop. Forcing herself to take slow, measured breaths, she waited for the computer to boot up.

When the last of the launch applications fired and the mouse acknowledged her guidance, she removed the cap from the flash drive and inserted it into the USB port. The laptop dinged, acknowledging the new hardware, then prompted Janie to view the files. Her heart fluttered as she clicked.

The folder revealed several numbered video files. The first was titled 1-Intro. Her hand trembled, causing the mouse cursor to jitter across the screen until it hovered over the file.

"Please, God," she whispered.

She double clicked the file, and the video played.

3

A moment of static, then a familiar face appeared. She recognized him immediately. It was Javy Romero. He smiled at the camera, showcasing shiny white teeth. Janie turned up the volume to drown out the pounding of her heart.

"My name is Javy Romero, and I have an opportunity for you."

Janie fought a wave of déjà vu. This was very familiar. The opening line down to the backwards red baseball cap and black t-shirt he wore scratched at her memory.

"I am an independent filmmaker, and this is an open call."

Now it clicked. It was the open call for the reality show. Mark found it online and showed it to her with great interest. At first, she was skeptical, but Mark's enthusiasm was contagious. By the end of the video, she fully supported his desire to audition.

"The world is full of mysteries. I want to see what happens when two people from different spectrums of belief coexist in a rumored place of supernatural power. The skeptic and the believer, spending a week in an abandoned mansion rumored to be a portal to other realms. I'm looking for two volunteers to join me at the Chamberlain Estate, where we will spend one week investigating the legends. Will we find the supernatural? Will we debunk the whole thing? Will clashing beliefs create an energy to serve as a battery for the unknown? We're going to find out, and I'm going to film it all. I will upload it to my channel for all to see. I'm offering five hundred dollars a night for this once in a lifetime experience. Part documentary, part character study, full on journey into the unknown. Send your audition videos to the email address listed in the comments and let me know why you should be part of The Battle of Belief!"

The video cut to a moment of dead air. Janie stared at the blue screen, her stomach twisting into knots. When the picture returned, she choked back a sob.

Mark smiled at her through the laptop screen. She knew exactly what he would say before he said a word. She had watched this video hundreds of times. It was the most recent video of Mark she possessed.

"Hi. My name is Mark Landon, and I'm the guy you need to solve the mysteries of the universe."

Warm tears ran down Janie's cheeks and she unconsciously reached a trembling hand toward the screen, as if she could feel him again. He laughed at his own joke, oozing with confidence, before continuing.

"I am a man of science, and I believe there's a logical explanation for any so-called *phenomenon* people encounter. I'm a physics major, so putting a trained eye on the unexplainable is right in my wheelhouse. Plus, I'm a people person. I get along with everybody. Ask anyone, they'll tell you." He beamed an exaggerated smile and then laughed again.

He was cheesy, but charming. His charisma was a magnet drawing you in and knocking down your defenses. It was one of the many reasons Janie had fallen for him—one of the many things she missed dearly.

He dropped the over the top charade and continued in a serious tone. "All jokes aside, this is an amazing opportunity. The experience will be invaluable. It's a chance to shed light on the possibilities of science and introduce people to a new way of thinking. I'd be honored to be a participant in The Battle of Belief."

The clip ended, and Janie fought the urge to stop the file and play it again. It took her back to all the nights she lay on the couch crying herself to sleep while the audition video played on repeat. Had the brief delay between videos lasted any longer, she would have given in and played it again. She knew the constant viewings were equivalent to a drug addiction pushing her deeper into the black hole of all-consuming depression, but she didn't give a shit.

A new video appeared on the screen, and she drew back. The face on screen was so ghastly white it had to be make-up. His hair was deep black, long and straight, parted down the middle and hanging around his face like black curtains. He reminded her of the goth kids she'd gone to high school with. He stared intensely at the camera with black eyes that were definitely contacts.

"Good evening," he said in a somber voice.

Janie chuckled despite everything. The man was a caricature.

"My name is Cain Murdoch. All my life, I have been a conduit between the living and the dead. Spirits called to me when I was but a mere child. Many secrets of the afterlife have been entrusted to my knowledge. Now, they call for me again. You claim the Chamberlain Estate is a place of great power.

You'll need an unbreakable connection to the other side to channel that energy. I can be that connection. Whoever you choose to accompany me on this journey will see things they thought impossible. I will make believers of everyone. You call it The Battle of Belief. The battle will be short-lived, for when the spirits make themselves known, there will be nothing left to question. I am the choice of the spirits. I trust I will meet you soon."

The man lowered his head, his dark hair closing around his face, and the screen faded to black. Janie stared at the screen, her forehead crinkled in amused fascination.

Another video clip started, revealing Javy Romero again. He smiled and waved at the camera.

"Welcome back! As promised, I'm documenting the complete experience, and that includes the audition process. You've just witnessed the audition videos for Mark and Cain. After viewing hundreds of submissions, they are my chosen participants. It wasn't easy narrowing it down with so many great options. In the end, these two won out. Mark is exactly what I'm looking for—smart guy, science background, easygoing, and likable. The last thing I want is to put two people together who don't get along and turn this into a trashy reality show. Cain, I mean, come on! He was the choice of the spirits after all. How could I not choose him? If anybody believes in ghosts and the beyond, it's this guy. So, the table is set. We leave in two days for the Chamberlain Estate. The cameras will roll, and we'll see what secrets are revealed. Stay tuned!"

The video ended. The reality of what could be on the other videos overwhelmed Janie. This could be the answer to everything. Adrenaline surged through her as she closed out the first video file and moused over a file titled 2-Pickup.

After all this time, she had hope. The words written in the

letter echoed in her mind. *Mark is not dead. Watch the videos. I need your help.*

The second video filled the laptop screen, and she pressed play.

4

The next scene began inside an airport. The camera swept across the cluttered terminal before settling on the escalator.

"We're at the airport picking up our researchers," Javy said from behind the camera. He tilted the lens down to a poster board propped up beside him with the names Mark and Cain written in big block letters. "No sign of them yet, but they should arrive any minute." He spun the camera around facing him and smiled. "I, for one, can't wait."

The video skipped and returned, again focused on the escalator. Mark stood at the top of the landing, a backpack thrown over one shoulder. He scanned the crowd of people waiting below, instantly noticing the camera and welcome sign. He flashed a beaming smile and threw up a wave.

Janie fought a lump in her throat. This was what she longed for. This was Mark after he kissed her goodbye and got on that plane.

"Here we go," Javy said. "Mark is in the house!"

He placed the camera on what Janie assumed was a tripod

and stepped into the frame. Mark worked through the crowd and offered his hand. Javy shook it and pulled him into a one-armed hug.

A bro hug, Janie mused. That's what Mark always called it.

"Welcome to Cincinnati, Mark."

Mark slapped his free hand across Javy's back. "Glad to be here. This is exciting, man. Can't wait to see this place. Am I the first one here? Looking forward to meeting my partner in crime." He looked again at the sign. "Cain, I assume?"

"Yeah, his name is Cain. I think you'll know him when you see him."

"Oh, yeah?"

"He definitely looks the part."

"Awesome. I'm gonna drop this here and go grab my other bag," Mark said. He slid the backpack from his shoulder, set it on the floor, and moved into the crowd towards the baggage claim.

Javy turned to the camera and gave two thumbs up. "I love him already!"

Janie smiled against the tears burning in her eyes. She knew the feeling. Mark's charisma was infectious. He could turn the tide of any conversation and instantly put people at ease. She didn't realize until he was gone how much of an anchor he was for her. He was her lighthouse in the storm, always there to guide her home. She felt herself slipping and took a deep, calming breath. Now was not the time to fall apart. Returning her focus to the video, she saw the camera aimed back at the escalator.

"Oh wow," Javy said. "Look at my man, Cain."

The man on the escalator was clearly Cain. The long black hair hanging around the pale face was undeniable. However, the audition video had not done justice to the man's size. He was a giant. Judging from the people around him, he was nearly seven feet tall. The other nearby airport patrons cast curious glances at him, but if he noticed or cared, he didn't let on.

"Oh, that has to be him," Mark said, stepping in front of the camera.

Javy laughed. "That's our boy."

Javy and Mark both waved at Cain. He acknowledged them with an almost imperceptible nod. The crowd parted, giving him a wide berth. He strode confidently toward the camera and stopped in front of the two men.

"Good Morning." He reached out and shook Javy's hand.

Javy pulled Cain into a hug, and he stiffened, clearly uncomfortable.

"Welcome, my friend. I'm Javy, and this is Mark. He will be your partner on our little adventure."

"Great to meet you, man," Mark said. He shook Cain's hand, but restrained himself from the bro hug, much to Cain's relief. "This is gonna be a blast. I'm excited to pick your brain about the paranormal and see how it jives with science."

"I am happy to introduce you to the world of spirits. I suspect you will leave this investigation a changed man."

Javy focused the camera on the two men.

"I suspect you are right, Cain. What we learn over the next week might surprise us both. I'm ready for anything."

"I hope that's true. You are confident in your belief, but I have seen the power of the spirits. Once you have seen the true nature of the spirit realm, science falters. There is much beyond the knowledge of man."

"You're right," Mark said. "Science is ever growing. We're only beginning to understand the world. I want to be on the leading edge. I want to prove the supernatural and paranormal are actually naturally occurring things that science has yet to identify."

Cain eyed Mark thoughtfully, then the corner of his mouth lifted in a smile. "I admire your enthusiasm and respect your opinion. You are halfway there. Where our beliefs separate is defining the paranormal. I believe that is why we are here, Mr. Romero?"

"Please, call me Javy. And yes, that is why we're here, and this is why I picked you guys. We haven't even left the airport, and you guys are already deep into philosophy. I love it!"

Mark laughed, and Cain smiled.

"Okay! Let's collect our things and hit the road. The Chamberlain Estate awaits!"

The camera cut away, and the video ended.

5

Despite her anxiousness to start the next video, Janie could no longer repress her need to pee. She raced out of the living room to the bathroom, silently cursing herself for such a mundane function, forcing her away from the still surreal videos waiting to be viewed. She stopped at the fridge on her way back through, hand jittering as she reached for a can of Monster, reconsidered, then opted for a beer. Chemically induced adrenaline probably wasn't the best idea right now. Alcohol would take the edge off, calm her down.

She returned to the couch, cracked open the Michelob Ultra, and downed half the can in one long drink. Warmth surged through her body at the sudden blast of alcohol. The head rush reminded her of her empty stomach. She took another swig, made a mental note to get some food later, grabbed the mouse, and clicked the next file.

The screen filled with the interior of a car. The video was being recorded on a phone mounted to the dashboard. Javy drove with Mark in the passenger seat and Cain crammed comically in the back. He leaned forward, the top of his head pressed against the ceiling.

"We are on the road to Chamberlain," Javy said to the camera. "Our participants Mark and Cain have arrived safely, and we are en route to our destination. Apologies for the limited headroom."

Cain grunted from the backseat. "It's not a problem. I find most things are not designed with tall people in mind."

"You sure you don't want the front?" Mark asked. "I know I called shotgun, but I'm a reasonable man."

"It's fine. I'm used to it, and the front is probably not any taller than the back. Also, I respect the laws of shotgun." Cain smiled as Mark burst into laughter.

"I love that you guys are getting along," Javy said. "I was afraid you two would butt heads right away, and this would be a waste of time. You've put me at ease."

"Don't sell yourself short," Mark said. "Credit where it's due. You chose your contestants wisely."

"I agree," Cain said. "I have no doubt in my abilities to converse with the spirits, and I'm relieved Mark is open to possibilities. There will be great debate when the spirits make themselves known. I look forward to it."

"That's what I'm here for," Mark replied. He reached his fist up behind him to the backseat and was pleased when Cain immediately bumped it back with his own. "This is gonna be awesome."

"Hell yeah, it's gonna be awesome," Javy said. "We've got about an hour drive time, so let me give you the history of the place."

"Sounds good. I did some research, but there is very little info online," Mark said.

"Likewise. I found that odd," Cain said. "I am well-versed in places labeled as paranormal hot spots, and I am not familiar with the Chamberlain Estate. If it has this reputation, I would think there would be a lot of discussion on the internet."

"You're both right. It's fairly well known locally, but the internet has turned a blind eye to it. I think we might change that here in a couple of weeks."

"Fill us in," Mark said.

"Lawrence Chamberlain built the house in 1831."

"That's significant," Cain announced.

"What is?"

"Built in 1831. Those digits add up to thirteen."

Mark repressed a smile. "Lucky number thirteen, right?"

"Popular culture has dubbed it so, but the number thirteen is significant. In tarot, the thirteenth card is Death."

"Oh, no," Mark said. "We're all doomed!"

Cain smiled, catching the *Friday the 13th* reference. "Not at all. The death card is commonly misinterpreted as a bad sign. Not the case. Death signifies major change. The death of one thing leads to the birth of another."

"I'm sure there were plenty of houses built in 1831. Are all of them haunted?"

"Of course not," Cain replied. "I'm not suggesting the house is haunted because it was built in 1831. It's just a noteworthy connection. I suspect there will be many more contributing factors. Javy, please, continue."

"So, yeah. Lawrence Chamberlain was a wealthy businessman with a bit of a bad reputation among his peers. The rumor was he spent a lot of his time studying the occult. No one went after him about it, because he was an intimidating man. People were afraid he might curse them if they crossed him. He made his fortune, then moved out of the city. After construction finished in the fall of 1831, Lawrence and his wife Sarah moved into the estate."

"Is this when the murders began?" asked Mark, feigning a look of horror.

"Actually, no," Javy answered. "Lawrence and Sarah lived out the rest of their lives in the house. They had two sons, Nathan and Daniel. Sarah died of the flu in 1860. Lawrence died shortly after, in 1862, from unknown causes."

"Unknown causes?" Cain leaned forward between the seats. "Foul play?"

"That's the thing. There's no record of any investigation, but the medical records are unusual. Lawrence seemed to be in excellent health, except he was dead."

"Interesting," Cain said.

"Keep in mind," Mark said, "this was the 1860s. There were tons of unknown medical conditions that are commonly diagnosed today. Who's to say he didn't die of perfectly natural causes and they hadn't classified the illness yet?"

Cain grunted an acknowledgement. "That's absolutely a possibility. Likely, even. Though you have already ruled out any connection to his dabblings with the occult. There's great power in that—dangerous power. It's completely possible Lawrence might have unlocked demonic forces in his practices, leading to his death."

Javy and Mark traded glances. Javy smiled at the playful smirk on Mark's face. Cain watched the exchange with an amused look.

"Come now, gentleman. I admitted the undiagnosed illness as a legitimate possibility. Keep an open mind to answers beyond the realm of science."

"Fair enough," Mark said. "My mind is open."

Javy chuckled from the driver's seat. "This is great."

Janie watched the conversation on the laptop screen with glazed eyes. She lost herself in the easy back and forth between the men the same way she often lost herself in many past conversations with Mark. The more she watched, the more memories flooded her mind. The sound of his voice was hypnotic, transporting her back to happier times.

"Anyway," Javy continued, "the Chamberlain sons kept the estate up throughout the years to equally little fanfare. They both married and raised families, living together in the house. All of them died from natural causes. And so it goes, for nearly two hundred years. The estate was never sold. It passed from generation to generation. Then, in a strange twist, the house was abandoned in 1988. Derek Chamberlain, the five times great grandson of Lawrence Chamberlain, had lived alone in the house since the death of his mother, Evelyn, ten years prior. Then, one day, he left. Derek set up directions and procedures for upkeep of the estate through his lawyers and completely dropped off the grid."

"So, hold up a minute," Mark said. "If Derek Chamberlain is off the grid, how are we investigating the house? We're not breaking in, right?"

"Derek Chamberlain *was* off the grid for over twenty years. A few weeks ago, he sent me a message."

6

Janie watched the exchange on screen with the same doubt visible on the faces of Mark and Cain. The idea of the estate owner basically missing since the late eighties would randomly message a YouTube creator seemed unlikely.

"He messaged you? You mean he emailed you?" Cain asked.

"Yeah," Javy answered. "I was doing early recon for this show, trying to find a place that hasn't been investigated a hundred times already. I put some inquiries out on the net, and he emailed me."

"Don't you think that's a little bizarre?" asked Mark.

"Not at first. I'd never heard of the place, so I didn't know anything about Derek Chamberlain. It was one of a handful of potential locations people suggested. Then I researched it and discovered the same thing you guys did. Not much to report. Certainly nothing to suggest it's a paranormal hot spot. I had to dig deep into property records to find anything. Chamberlains all the way back to the beginning. That sent me down a rabbit hole of old news articles and ancestry records. Once I had the whole story, or at least what's public record, I was hooked. I flew to Ohio and drove out here to interview the locals. The house is in the country, miles from any neighbors, so there wasn't a lot to learn. Everybody knew of the place, and there were vague stories of occult shenanigans, but everyone I spoke to seemed content to leave it alone."

"That's intriguing," said Cain. "A local place with that history should be a magnet to teenagers looking for a thrill as well as ghost hunting organizations. Based on your descriptions, it almost sounds like the locals are afraid to go near it."

"Agreed. That's why I picked it. Whatever the story is here, I want to uncover it."

"Hold up, fellas," Mark said. "Let's get back to this email from Derek Chamberlain. What exactly did it say?"

"It was very formal, business-like. He said it had come to his attention that I was in search of potentially haunted locations for a documentary, and offered access to the Chamberlain Estate. He said it was his family's historical home, and he himself had encountered many strange events while growing up there. I said I would do some research and consider the offer. I wrote him back a couple of days later and said it was perfect."

Mark gazed at Javy thoughtfully, and Janie knew he was thinking the same thing she was. Based on the history Javy discovered, it felt very suspicious for this Chamberlain guy to contact an unknown documentary filmmaker to investigate his house. It didn't sit right with her, and she could tell Mark felt the same way.

"This sounds sketchy to me. I don't know, it just feels odd. Why would this guy do this? From what you say, the family was extremely private and kept to themselves. It's weird."

"I agree," Cain said.

Javy shifted uncomfortably in the driver's seat and cleared

his throat. "I know it seems pretty random, but the more I read about the history and rumors, I knew it had to be this place. Besides, I've emailed back and forth with Derek several times getting this all arranged, and he seems like a completely normal dude. He's actually meeting us there to let us in. You guys will get to judge for yourselves. I'm on the record saying I trust him."

The three men slipped into silence. Javy appeared frazzled by the questioning. Mark and Cain both appeared deep in thought, gazing out the windows at the corn and soybean fields rolling past. It was the first time Janie sensed any discomfort from Mark and it made her nervous. Mark was never uncomfortable, always in control and quick to adjust. The concern on his face was foreign to her. She wanted to scream at the computer, tell them to stop the car and go back. But it was too late for that.

Or was it? Again, she thought of the note.

Mark is not dead.

Javy cleared his throat and pointed ahead.

"There it is. The Chamberlain Estate."

7

The camera bounced erratically as Javy pulled it from the holder on the dashboard and spun it around to the windshield.

"Would you mind filming this for me?" Javy asked.

"Sure," Mark answered, taking the camera and fixing the lens on the Chamberlain Estate.

Even with several trees blocking sections of the house, it was obviously massive. A wrought-iron fence ran the length of the property, disappearing behind the structure. The entry gate was open, and Javy turned onto the paved driveway. As they approached the house, the drive split—the right path disappearing around the back, the left circling into a roundabout in the front. A shiny black Lexus sat parked in the circle drive near the front door. Javy pulled up behind it and shut off the engine.

"Wow, what a mansion!" Mark said, then twisted in his seat and swiveled his head back and forth between Javy and Cain, grinning with anticipation.

Cain smiled, picking up the reference. "What? What is this?"

Mark busted out laughing and threw a high five to Cain. "My man!"

Janie laughed despite herself, watching them joke on the video. She wasn't a gamer herself, but she had spent countless hours on the couch with Mark while he played. Resident Evil was his favorite, and he never missed an opportunity to use one of the infamous lines of cheesy dialog.

Javy chuckled. "Okay, STARS Unit. Let's do this thing. This is our guy."

The door of the Lexus opened, and a man stepped out. He wore black dress pants and a button-up shirt, hair pulled back in a tight ponytail, and sunglasses covering his eyes. He gave a pleasant smile and waved at the group.

Javy snatched the camera from Mark and got out of the car. The screen bounced and focused on the blacktop driveway. Janie heard two more car doors close and knew Mark and Cain had joined him.

"Mr. Chamberlain, I presume?" Javy asked. "You don't mind if I film, do you?"

"Of course not," the man answered, "and please, call me Derek."

He reached out a hand, and Javy shook it.

"Awesome. Thank you so much for having us. These are my investigators, Mark and Cain."

Both men stepped into view and took turns shaking hands.

"Pleasure to meet you all."

"This is an impressive home you have, sir," Mark said. He gazed up at the house.

"Thank you. It's been our family home for over two hundred years, as I'm sure you are aware."

"If you'll forgive my bluntness," Cain said, "why are you

allowing us to investigate your home? Based on all accounts, your family has held privacy in high regard. It seems unusual, after all these years, the family would let strangers investigate and film inside."

"I understand it may seem unlike us, based on the history, but I am the only Chamberlain left. I have had experiences here that defy all logic. Frankly, I want to validate my experiences. I do not share the need for privacy my parents and grandparents had. I want answers."

"Why us?" asked Mark.

Javy shuffled his feet, clearly uncomfortable. "What he means is, what led you to choosing my channel as a medium to investigate and tell the story?"

"I could have gone a more traditional route, maybe a research group at one of the colleges. That brings with it a lot of red tape and headache. I wanted to move quickly and off the grid with this. I'm fine broadcasting the results. I just didn't want to jump through a dozen hoops. I came across your channel, and was impressed with your past work."

Javy beamed at the compliment.

"Why did you leave?" Mark asked.

"Leave?"

"Yeah, why did you leave? Javy told us you left the house in 1988. You've been gone a long time."

"Oh, of course," Derek replied. "Sometimes I forget it's been that long. Honestly, I didn't feel right staying in this big house alone after my parents died. There have always been multiple Chamberlains living here. I wasn't comfortable staying here alone."

"I understand," Mark said. "That's a lot of house for one man to keep up."

"Indeed. Unfortunately, I have to be going. I have other obligations to tend to. I'm sure you have many questions. I've left a file in the library with notes and recollections of past events in the house. I suspect it will give you plenty to go on."

He reached into his pocket, removed a set of keys, and handed them Javy.

"Here are keys to all the exterior doors, as well as the barn and gate. We generally have no issues with trespassers, but as a precaution, I still suggest you lock the gate after I leave. Should you need me, you have my number."

Derek made his way to the car, then turned back. "Good luck. I look forward to seeing what you discover." He smiled, then dropped into the car.

"Thank you for the opportunity," Javy called out. "We won't let you down."

Derek circled the car around the drive, waving at the men as he passed, and then disappeared into the trees along the twisting path. The sound of the motor faded until only the sound of birds chirping and the crunch of gravel underfoot remained.

Javy focused the camera on Mark and Cain, then jingled the keys in front of the lens. "Okay, guys. It's go time."

8

Despite the pristine condition of the outside, Janie imagined the interior to be dark and gloomy, cobwebs swaying on silent breezes, agonizing groans emanating from the floorboards with every step.

When the video returned, she jolted forward in her seat. Rather than footage of the three men entering the Chamberlain Estate, a close-up shot of Javy in a darkened room appeared. His usual tan complexion had been replaced with a pale gray. His clean-shaven face now featured dark stubble, and his eyes were bloodshot and puffy. Had she not spent the last couple hours watching film footage of him, she doubted she would have recognized him at all.

"If you're seeing this video, then you got my package, and you've watched the beginning footage." His voice was deeper than before, dry and unused. "Like I said in the note, Mark is not dead. I know it's been months, but you have to believe me when I say if I could have reached you sooner, I would have."

Janie gazed at the screen, hanging on to every word, waiting for Javy to say something that made sense—something to make everything finally click together. Javy paused, clearly uncomfortable in his surroundings.

"I'm stopping you here, because what happened next, after we went inside, is going to be hard to believe. I wouldn't believe it myself if I hadn't been there." He paused and dropped his head into his hands. A faint squeaking sound offscreen caused him to jerk upright and scan the room. His breathing came in erratic bursts and sweat gathered on his brow. "I have to move soon. I think they're close again. Janie, listen to me. I need your help. I have the rest of the footage, but I won't let it out of my sight. I hope we can save Mark, but I'll need you to help me, and I need you to see what happened—what's still happening. Mark told me once about a coffee shop you two love to visit. I won't say the name in case this video falls into the wrong hands. I will look for you there every night at seven. If I don't see you, I'm gone. I can't stay in one place. I have to keep moving. I know you have questions, and I'll answer everything I can when we're together. For now, I need you to trust me. I need your help. Mark needs your help. I hope to see you soon, before it's too late."

Javy stared into the camera for a moment, his bloodshot eyes glistening with tears, then he reached forward and switched it off. The screen went black and the video file ended.

Janie leaned back and closed her eyes. Her mind flooded with questions. What happened in that house? If Mark was alive, where was he and why hadn't he come to her? Who or what was Javy running from? His instructions ran through her mind. The coffee shop. She knew exactly which one. Candy's. Mark had asked her out for coffee shortly after they met, and Candy's was his favorite place to get a cup of joe. She fell in love with the place instantly—the garish pink siding, the stage set up by the front bay window for acoustic acts and open mic nights, the smell of coffee grounds floating over the buzz of conversation; all of it enraptured her. It was the perfect setting to begin a whirlwind fairy tale romance. They fell for each other quickly, and Candy's became a staple. She hadn't been since Mark left for the show, and the thought of going back without him twisted her stomach into knots.

She was desperate for answers and to find Mark if he wasn't gone, but she was also terrified. The world had become a dark place and the thought of going back into the fray, back to Candy's, put her on the edge of panic. How could she trust Javy? Mark had gone away with him and never came back. What if Javy was a psycho, killed Mark and Cain, and now wanted her? What did she really know about him? Then the image of him staring at the camera in the last video returned. He didn't look like a man trying to trick a girl. He looked desperate and afraid.

She squinted at the microwave clock on the kitchen counter and made out 11:37. Javy had said seven o'clock. Seven hours until he would be at Candy's looking for her. She had to go, but not alone. There was only one person to go with her, and she shuddered at the thought of making the call. Things had not gone well last time they spoke, and Janie wasn't sure she would even answer. Still, she was the only choice. This was too big not to include her, and there was no one else to ask.

Janie took a deep breath to calm her nerves and picked up her phone. She scrolled through the contacts until she found the name. Leslie Landon. The picture of the smiling girl, who shared many of the same facial features as her brother, stared back at Janie, sending a stab of guilt through her. She chewed her lip nervously, working up the courage to make the call.

Before it's too late.

Janie gritted her teeth and sent the call.

PART TWO

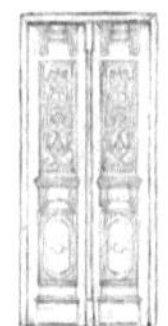

I

Leslie Landon sat at her desk, watching people pass her door to the steady drone of office noise. Muffled phone conversations and clacking keyboards created a white noise effect, lulling her to the brink of sleep. She took a sip of lukewarm coffee and returned her focus to the twin computer monitors on her desk.

One monitor displayed a spreadsheet of monthly sales reports. The other showed a search engine display of hospitals in southwest Ohio. A pad of paper lay on the desk next to her, with hospital names and numbers scribbled in her frantic handwriting.

She glanced at the office door to ensure no one was coming, then returned to her search. In the months since her brother disappeared, calling hospitals and police stations had become an obsession. She felt the local authorities had given up too easily. The police didn't have a lot of information. They knew Mark flew to Cincinnati to meet with a filmmaker named Javy Romero. There was also supposed to be a third person involved in the project, but his identity was unknown. The casting call video cited the filming location as the Chamberlain Estate. The police contacted the owner, who claimed the group of investigators stayed on the property for a week, then left on schedule. A search of the house turned up no evidence. A canvas of the nearby town produced no leads. No one claimed to have seen the men investigating the house. After a couple of weeks of dead ends, the case went cold.

Leslie could not live with that. Missing person cases may be common to law enforcement, but her missing brother was not something she could let go. Mark was her only sibling, and only a year older than her. He was her big brother, but throughout their lives, she had been the more mature child, keeping her adventurous brother under her wing. They were very close as children, and that bond continued into adulthood. There was an unbreakable connection between them, and she felt it with all her soul that Mark was alive. She could not accept the possibility he was gone. Not until she found him.

As the days and weeks passed by, she continued to follow up with hospitals and police stations in a widening arc around the Chamberlain house. There had to be something—a clue, a witness. He couldn't have vanished off the face of the earth. He was out there, and she would do everything she could to find him, even if she was on her own.

Doing it on her own was the part that stung most. She understood the police couldn't put endless resources on a case with no leads, but Janie should help her. Leslie knew if anyone loved Mark more than her, it was Janie. When Mark and Janie started dating, Leslie approved right away. Janie was a sweet girl and a perfect match for Mark. With their parents both gone, Leslie was the only family Mark had, and it was important his partner be someone she trusted. Janie proved herself to be everything Leslie hoped for, and the two of them had gotten as close as sisters. When Mark went missing, Leslie was not prepared for Janie to shut down.

Janie was grieving Mark before she knew for sure he was gone. To Leslie, it felt like betrayal. Had the situation been reversed, Mark would search the ends of the earth for Janie. To think Janie could just lay down and die with him infuriated Leslie. After a few weeks of trying to rouse Janie and get her involved, Leslie had given up. That made the hurt even worse. She was missing her brother, and now she was missing the one person who should have been by her side to see this through.

As she gazed at the monitor, a knock snapped her to attention. She quickly hit alt-tab on the keyboard to minimize the search engine and turned to the door.

"Hey Leslie, a bunch of us are going out for lunch. You want to come?"

She sighed, relieved it was Marie from accounting and not her boss. "Yeah, sure. I'll meet you in the lobby."

"Sounds good," Marie said before turning back down the hall.

Leslie locked her computer and grabbed her purse. Some time out of the office and away from the search would be good for her. It was nearly impossible for her to turn off her brain. She felt guilty any time she allowed herself a moment to clear her mind when she knew Mark was out there and needed help. She vowed to get back to the search and make more calls as soon as she got back from lunch.

She made it to her office door when her cell phone rang. She stopped and pulled the phone from her purse. Her blood ran cold when she saw the name on the caller ID.

Janie.

In a flash, the last conversation she had with Janie flooded back. She stopped by Mark and Janie's house after her last several calls and texts had gone unanswered. She found Janie curled up on the couch. The house was a disaster, and Janie had not been eating, showering, or making any effort to do anything. She thought of the countless hours she'd spent trying to find any kind of lead on Mark, and seeing Janie dead to the world and doing nothing sent her over the edge. She screamed at Janie to get her shit together and stop being such a flake. How could she give up on Mark? He would never give up on her. Janie lay on the couch, sobbing weakly into a pillow. Leslie left the house in a rage and hadn't bothered to reach out again.

Now, with Janie's name flashing on her phone, she assumed the worst. What if the police had finally found him—found his body? Her heart thudded in her chest and nausea wracked her. She closed her eyes and took a steadying breath, felt the dull vibration of the phone in her hands, then accepted the call.

2

"Hello?"

There was a long pause.

"What is it, Janie? What happened?" She paused for a moment as she prepared herself for the news. "Did they find him?"

"No," Janie answered, "but I got a package in the mail, and I need you to see it."

Leslie frowned. "What kind of package? Listen, Janie, if this isn't about finding Mark, then honestly, I don't have time for your shit." She grimaced at the harshness of her tone, but couldn't help herself. The anger she still felt towards Janie boiled over when she heard her voice.

"It is about Mark. Leslie, I'm sorry. I know I let you down. I let Mark down. But we have a chance now. I think I know how to find him."

"Okay, I'm sorry for snapping at you. Tell me what's going on."

"I got a package in the mail with a flash drive. There was a note. It said Mark's not dead, and to watch the videos, and that he needed help."

"Who is he? Who sent it to you? What videos?" Leslie felt her hands shaking as adrenaline pumped through her veins.

"Javy sent it."

"Javy Romero, the filmmaker?" Leslie's heart leapt in her chest. Javy was also missing. If he was alive, it meant maybe Mark was too. "What was the video?"

"The flash drive had footage for the show up to them arriving at the Chamberlain Estate. I need you to come. Javy asked me to meet him, and I'm afraid to do it alone. You'll understand when you see the videos. I just, I need you to come."

Leslie's mind swirled with uncertainty as she considered everything Janie was saying. "What does it show? Does it show what happened to him?"

"No. Javy said he would show me the rest, but he wants to meet me. You'll understand when you see it. Please, just come."

"Okay, I'm coming. I'm leaving work now. I'll be there in an hour. Should we call the cops?"

"No, I don't think so. Not yet, anyway. Just come and see."

"Okay, I'm on my way." Leslie ended the call and made for the elevator. As she rode down the ten floors to the lobby level, she typed a quick text to her boss that she had a family emergency and had to leave. In the lobby, a group of coworkers gathered in a circle, waiting for Leslie.

"You ready?" Marie asked.

"I'm sorry, I have an emergency. I have to go. Next time," Leslie called out as she blew past the group. She heard Marie ask what happened, but didn't bother to answer. She pushed through the revolving door onto the sidewalk and made for the parking garage next door.

Her thoughts swirled at the possibilities of what this could mean. Scenarios flashed through her mind. Whatever it was, it was a lead, the first one since this whole thing started. For the first time since the disappearance, there was a light at the end of the tunnel.

She made her way to the rear of the parking garage to her Camry and dropped into the seat, tossing her purse to the side. As she weaved through the narrow pathway through the garage, she briefly considered calling Jared, but decided against it. He wasn't expecting her soon. No need to get him involved until she knew what she was dealing with.

She scanned her parking pass at the gate and pulled out into traffic, glancing at the clock on the dashboard. It was noon, and she hoped the lunchtime traffic wouldn't slow her down. The radio played softly, and she turned it off. Her mind was scrambled enough without the droning commentary of the radio host.

Three months since Mark disappeared. Three months of wondering what could have happened. Leslie had thought through so many options. She always came back to the same conclusion. Someone had taken him. There was no way he would leave on his own. He loved Janie too much, and the bond between him and his sister was unbreakable.

Now, with the city dwindling behind her, she was on the way to finally getting answers. She pushed the gas pedal harder as the highway opened up, knuckles white and bulging on the steering wheel. She could feel the weight of it all around her. Everything was about to change.

3

Forty-five minutes later, Leslie whipped the Camry into the driveway beside Janie's old Alero. She wrinkled her nose in disgust at the state of the place. The grass was nearly knee deep in places, and bags of trash lined the edge of the house. The obvious neglect sent another flare of resentment through her. Janie gave up on the place, just like she gave up on Mark. She took a calming breath and gritted her teeth. Now wasn't the time to be hostile, not when they finally had a lead.

She steeled herself for an uncomfortable greeting and climbed out of the car. Before she got to the steps, the screen door swung open and Janie stepped out onto the porch. The two women stared at each other for a moment, neither knowing how to break the ice. Then Janie lurched forward, jumped down the stairs, and wrapped Leslie up in a fierce hug. Leslie stiffened in surprise, then reluctantly hugged her back.

"I'm sorry, Leslie," Janie sobbed. "I'm sorry I wasn't there for you. You were hurting as much as I was, and I wasn't there. I'm so sorry."

A flash of rage boiled in Leslie, but then she felt her own eyes burn with tears and before she could stop herself, emotion overtook her and she sobbed along with Janie. Despite everything, it felt good to hug her friend again.

"Let's go inside," Leslie said as she released Janie and wiped her eyes. "Show me what you've got."

Janie nodded and led the way inside. Leslie followed her through the familiar hallway and kitchen to the living room. She saw the laptop sitting open on the coffee table. Janie sat on the couch and motioned for Leslie to sit beside her.

"Okay, I'm going to play it all again. I want you to see everything I saw."

"Yeah, play it," Leslie said. Her heart raced as she watched Janie reach out and click the file. Her stomach fluttered like she was teetering on top of a roller coaster hill before plunging down the track.

Janie clicked through each file. Leslie had seen the casting call video only once when Mark sent it to her. In the time since the disappearance, she gathered all the information she could find on Javy Romero. There wasn't much. He was new to the filmmaking scene. His YouTube channel featured a couple dozen videos. They were entertaining, and she saw the potential for future success. His documentary on the paranormal might have been the break he was working towards had it not gone terribly wrong. There was nothing to suggest Javy was involved in some sort of sinister kidnapping. Leslie decided quickly Javy was a victim, the same as Mark.

Mark's audition hit her with a powerful wave of emotion. Her heart broke to see him full of life and excited. That was Mark as he always was. Her face flushed, and she closed her eyes to battle the tears she knew were coming.

When the image of Cain filled the screen, her gaze intensified. This was a new face, and she immediately grew suspicious. She fought the urge to judge a book by its cover, but this guy looked sketchy.

Janie must have sensed her uneasiness. "I know what you're thinking, but give it time."

Leslie nodded, but could not put away the idea that Cain had something to do with this.

She sat silently through the next couple of videos, watching as Javy picked up Mark and Cain at the airport, then the drive to the Chamberlain Estate. Only when Derek Chamberlain himself stepped out of the car did she show any reaction. The banter between Mark and Cain put her at ease and lessened her suspicions of the strange man. Now, as the mysterious owner of the house briefly chatted with the men, her suspicions flared up again.

"I don't trust him," she said.

"Chamberlain?"

"Yes. That guy is like a ghost. I can't find anything on him beyond the police report stating they talked to him. He said they left, and the cops searched the house, but it was too clean. I tried to contact him myself, but couldn't get to him."

"Keep watching, this is almost the end," Janie said as the men walked towards the front door.

When Javy appeared disheveled and desperate, Leslie tensed and leaned closer to the screen. She listened to his plea that Janie meet him at the coffee shop for the rest of the footage. When the screen went black, she exhaled a deep breath she didn't realize she was holding.

"Holy shit."

"Yeah," Janie answered, "holy shit."

"What the fuck happened in that house?"

"I don't know." Janie turned and grabbed Leslie's hand. "Will you go with me? I have to go, but I'm afraid to go by myself."

"Fuck yes, I'm going with you," Leslie said, almost shouting. She stood up and paced around the living room. She slid her phone out of the back pocket of her jeans and tapped the screen. "Jesus, we've still got six hours to kill. Okay, you get ready, and I'll meet you back here in a couple of hours. I'm gonna go home and get Jared so he can see the videos."

"Jared? Do you think that's a good idea?"

"We don't know what the fuck we're getting ourselves into, Janie. Jared is absolutely coming with us. Javy said nothing on the video about coming alone. You saw him. He looked terrified. I don't know what's going on, but I think we need all the help we can get."

"What about the cops? Do you think we should call them?"

Leslie considered, then shook her head. "Not yet. This is too weird, and if we show up at the coffee shop with a bunch of cops, Javy might run. We can't risk that happening. We wait until we know what's going on, then if we need the cops, we'll call them."

Janie nodded. She stood and followed Leslie back through the house. When they reached the door, Leslie turned and faced her.

"We're going to find him. I can feel it. You feel it too, don't you?" Leslie asked.

A single tear streaked down Janie's face, and she wiped it away. "I do."

"Good. I'll be back soon."

She hugged Janie briefly, then went out onto the porch. The sun was high and the air warm. Birds chirped in the tree beside the porch. Leslie sucked in a lung full of fresh air. The world felt more alive than it had in months. She climbed into her car and backed down the driveway. As she pulled away, she saw Janie still standing in the screen door. She waved at her, then drove away, hope surging through her veins.

4

Three hours later, Leslie pulled back into Janie's driveway with her bewildered boyfriend, Jared, in the passenger seat. She found him napping on the couch when she got home. In a flurry of energy, she shook him awake and unloaded the events of the afternoon. As the grogginess wore off, he tried to decipher everything Leslie told him. He had a lot of questions, but based on the intensity coming from Leslie, he opted not to press her.

Leslie filled the thirty-minute drive from her apartment to Janie's house with a barrage of theories, each more sinister than the one before it. Jared humored her and nodded tentative agreement, though he considered nearly all of them to be far-fetched. He had his own theories, though he learned early on to keep them to himself. To Jared, there was only one possibility. Mark had taken off. The one time he tried to pitch it to Leslie, she had shut him down with authority.

As they exited the car, Janie once again opened the screen door and met them on the porch. Leslie was relieved to see

Janie had showered and brushed her hair. She looked more put together than Leslie had seen her in weeks. It gave her hope.

"Hey, Janie. Good to see you," Jared said as he climbed the steps to the porch. He gave her a brief hug.

"Good to see you, too."

"Pretty crazy stuff we got here."

"Pretty crazy doesn't do it justice," Leslie said. She stepped past them and dragged Jared into the house by his shirtsleeve. "Come see for yourself. We've got time."

Janie started the videos for Jared, then followed Leslie into the kitchen. She made them each a cup of coffee with her Keurig, and they sat at the table.

"So here's what I'm thinking," Leslie said. "We go to the coffee shop and wait for Javy to show up. Jared stays with us. I'm not taking any chances. We'll hear him out and see what else he can tell us."

"And what else he can *show* us? He said he's got more footage. We need to see it."

"Yes. If he's got more video, then we cannot let him leave without giving it to us." Leslie looked at the clock on the oven. "Couple more hours. I say we get there early. Can't take a chance on missing him."

Janie nodded, then the two fell into an uncomfortable silence broken only by the sounds of the videos playing in the living room. They sipped coffee and traded glances at each other.

The tension broke when Jared stepped into the kitchen. He ran a hand through his hair and leaned against the counter.

"Well, what do you think?" Leslie asked.

"I think you girls are getting played."

Leslie frowned, disapproval radiating from her face. "Played?"

Jared nodded. "I think this Javy guy is trying to pull something over on you."

"I don't think so," Janie said. "You saw him in that last video. He looked scared."

"So he's a good actor. I'm telling you, this guy is up to no good. I don't know what happened to Mark. Maybe this guy killed him and now he's fucking with you guys."

"You shut the fuck up," Leslie growled. "Mark is not dead."

Jared, sensing the line of fire he stepped in, put up his hands in surrender. "I'm sorry, babe. I shouldn't have said that. We don't know what happened. All I'm saying is I don't trust this guy, and I think we need to be very careful."

"We will be careful, and we're going to get answers," Leslie said. She stared at Jared long enough to let him know he wasn't off the hook, then turned to Janie. "Let's get out of here. I can't stand to sit and wait anymore. We'll take our time getting there and get a table. Who knows, maybe he'll show up early. It might give us a chance to see him coming or see if anything seems suspicious."

"The whole thing is suspicious," Jared said.

Before Leslie could snap at him again, Janie cut in.

"I know it is, but it's all we've got. I have to see this through."

"Me too," Leslie said.

Jared nodded. "I know. We'll see it through. I promise to keep an open mind, but I've got my eye on this guy."

"Fair enough," Janie said. "Let's go."

The three of them gathered their things and walked outside. It was only five o'clock, but already the sun sank low in the sky, dropping the temperature along with it. They loaded up into Leslie's car and drove away. None of them noticed the black Lexus parked half a block down the street that pulled out after them.

5

Leslie pulled her Camry into one of the parking spots lining the side of the road. The pink siding of Candy's Coffee House stood out from the other buildings. Twilight had taken over the sky, and the warm glow of lights from inside painted the sidewalk. A small group of people stood outside smoking cigarettes. Leslie scanned their faces from a distance, but none of them resembled Javy.

"Let's get a table," Leslie said.

The group of smokers stepped aside as they passed. Jared pulled open the heavy wooden door and let the girls go ahead. The pleasant fragrance of coffee grounds greeted them. Leslie scanned the shop as they walked through the narrow aisle between tables. The evening crowd was arriving. A quick count gave her twelve customers either seated at tables or loitering around the counter. A couple of teenage boys were up on the small stage by the window tuning acoustic guitars. A small sign by the stage announced Open-Mic Night from seven to ten.

"I think we should set up in the back," Janie whispered.

Leslie nodded and led their group to an open table nestled in the back corner of the shop. From here they had a clear view of the building and entrance.

"I'll grab us some drinks," Jared said.

While Jared waited at the counter to order coffees, Leslie studied Janie. She worried how much she could count on Janie if things got crazy. She knew Janie cared deeply for Mark, but Leslie still couldn't let go of how quickly she'd given up.

"You okay?" Leslie asked.

Janie had been nervously scanning the room, her knee bouncing steadily. "I don't know."

"I need you to be on your game."

"I know," Janie answered. "It's weird being back here. I've never been here without him." She paused, then looked Leslie in the eyes. "I'll be okay. I have to be."

Leslie held her gaze for a moment, then nodded. She wanted to believe her, but until Janie proved herself reliable, she would prepare for the worst.

Jared returned carrying three cups of coffee. He passed them out, then sat on the stool. They sipped in silence, casting nervous glances at the door every few seconds. Leslie checked her phone. Fifteen minutes until seven.

"I'm gonna step outside and see if I see this guy coming," Jared said. "I'm keeping an open mind, but I'm still suspicious. If he shows up with a car full of thugs waiting outside to bag us as we come out, I want to know about it. He doesn't know who I am, so I shouldn't raise any alarms to him."

Leslie considered, then agreed. "Yeah, that's not a bad idea. Just don't spook him. If you see him, don't look at him twice, and definitely don't say anything to him. When he comes in, don't follow right away. We may not get another chance if he bails."

"I got it," Jared said. "Play it cool and blend in." He picked up his coffee and made his way back to the front of the store, past the young musicians now working through a sound check.

Leslie watched as he exited the shop and drifted past the bay window. She took another sip of her coffee and noticed her hands were shaking. She thought briefly of starting up a conversation with Janie, but quickly rejected the idea. Janie seemed content to sit in silence and wait it out.

At seven o'clock, as the boys onstage tore into a Nirvana song, Leslie's phone chirped with a text message. She snatched it from the table and unlocked the screen.

Jared: There's a dude across the street on the edge of the building. Came out of the alley. It's dark over there. Can't make out if it's him or not.

Leslie: Don't look at him.

Jared: I'm not. I'm looking at my phone :)

Leslie rolled her eyes, then handed her phone to Janie. Her eyes widened as she read the text.

"Stay cool, Janie. Stay cool."

Janie nodded, then took several shallow quick breaths, her eyes glued to the door of the coffee shop.

Jared: He's crossing the street now. He's got his hood up and head down, so I can't see his face, but I think it's him.

"Here we go," Leslie said.

The two girls gazed at the front of the shop. The door swung open, and a man entered. He wore a black hoodie with the hood pulled up. It was oversized, and the hood hung low over his face. A few of the coffee shop patrons eyed him nervously as he passed through the room. He passed the counter and made directly for their table. When he reached them, he stopped and pulled the hood down, revealing pale skin and frightened eyes.

"Janie, you came."

6

Leslie kept her face blank and motioned for Javy to sit.

He scanned the coffee shop, then lowered himself onto the stool.

"I'm Leslie, Mark's sister."

"I see the resemblance," Javy said.

"Let's skip the pleasantries and get to it," Leslie said. "Where is Mark? I've seen the videos you sent Janie. You said he's alive and you need help. Start talking."

Javy looked from Leslie to Janie, then back to Leslie, quickly recognizing her as the leader of the pair. He inhaled deeply, then let it out as if clearing his mind. "He's in the house."

"The cops searched the house. They didn't find anything."

"There are a lot of places you can go in Chamberlain," Javy said. He gazed at the table, his expression lost as if he were floating away. "Lots of places to hide if you don't want to be found."

"What the fuck does that mean?" Leslie felt her patience slipping. She didn't have time for riddles.

Leslie's hostility snapped Javy back to attention, and his

face flushed. "I'm sorry. You don't understand yet. You haven't seen the other videos. I keep forgetting that. I keep forgetting a lot."

Sensing Leslie was about to snap, Janie seized the moment and put her hand over Javy's on the table. Javy looked up at her and his eyes brimmed with tears.

"Tell us what happened," Janie said.

"I could tell you, but it wouldn't be enough. It's impossible to explain. You would think I'm a lunatic."

"Okay," Janie replied. "Do you have the rest of the videos? Can you give them to us?"

Javy stiffened. "I have them, but they stay with me. You have to see them, but I'm coming with you."

Leslie slipped her phone below the table and subtly sent a text to Jared. A moment later, the coffee shop door opened and Jared moved quickly toward their table.

Javy turned and tensed noticeably at the sight of Jared.

"It's okay. He's with us," Janie said.

Jared reached the table and sat on the unoccupied stool beside Leslie.

"You must be Javy."

Javy looked nervously from Jared to Janie.

"He's Leslie's boyfriend," she said.

Javy studied Jared for a moment, then his shoulders dropped, and he relaxed back onto the stool. "I thought you were with him."

"With who?" Leslie asked.

"You'll see when you watch the videos."

"You're going to have to give us a little more before we let you tag along. You're telling me Mark is still at the Chamberlain house, even though the police searched the place and found nothing, and even though it's been three months since he went there. That doesn't make sense. What's he been doing, hanging out?" Leslie shook her head. "I'm not buying it."

"I know it sounds crazy. If I hadn't been there and seen the things I've seen, I wouldn't believe it either."

"Is he being held captive?" Jared asked.

Javy hesitated as he considered the question. "Not exactly."

"I don't believe that," Janie said fiercely. "If he was free to leave, he would have come home. He would've come back to me."

"You're right. He's not being held captive like you mean," Javy said, nodding at Jared. "Something happened to him, and he's different now."

"Different how?" Leslie asked.

"You need to see. I know how weird it sounds. I know you don't trust me, and I don't blame you. For Mark's sake, give me a chance to show you. I think time is running out. We need to do something soon, or it will be too late."

"Fine," Jared said. "Give us the videos."

"He won't," Leslie answered. "He said he has to come with us."

Jared frowned and stared suspiciously at Javy.

"Please," Javy begged. "It's the only way." He twisted in his chair as the coffee shop door opened again. A small group of teenage girls piled into the shop, apparently fans of the boys on stage. Javy turned back to them. "We've got to move. They'll find me soon."

"Who's after you?" Leslie demanded. "Who are you afraid of? The police?"

Javy snorted. "I wish it was. Please, let's go. I'll show you the rest of the videos, and you can see for yourself."

"What choice do we have?" Janie asked the group.

Leslie stared at Javy, then nodded reluctantly. "If you're messing with us, it won't end well for you."

"Not at all," Jared said.

"I promise. You'll see, but we have to go."

"Let's go," Leslie said. She stood up, signaling the rest of the group to follow, and hurried through the coffee shop. Javy stopped them at the door.

"You go first and look around for anyone suspicious," Javy said.

"You're the only suspicious guy I see around here," Jared replied.

"I'm serious."

"Fine." Jared stepped out and looked up and down the street. He turned back to the door and waved them out. They rushed down the block to Leslie's car and piled in. Jared gave the front seat to Janie so he could sit in the back and keep an eye on Javy.

As Leslie pulled the car into traffic and made the turn to go back to Janie's house, she watched Javy in the rearview mirror, twisting in his seat and scanning the passing cars and sidewalks.

What the fuck have we gotten ourselves into?

7

A light rain fell as Leslie pulled into Janie's driveway. The ride had been awkwardly quiet, with Javy fidgeting nervously in his seat. They piled out of the car and into the house, Jared holding the door for them as they entered. Javy hovered in the hall near the screen door, scanning the street until Jared closed the front door and locked it.

"Relax, man," Jared said, giving Javy a gentle push down the hallway.

They gathered in the kitchen, and Leslie broke the ice.

"Let's see it then."

Javy nodded and pulled a flash drive from his front pocket.

"Before we do this, I need you guys to know that I have not tampered with this. Everything on here is real."

"I believe you," Janie replied.

The others turned to look at her.

"None of this has made any sense, so I don't expect whatever is on those videos to be any different. Something strange has happened. We can all agree on that. Let's see it through."

Leslie nodded and pointed toward the living room.

Javy led the way, plopping down onto the couch in front of the laptop. He removed the flash drive already inserted, and snapped in the new one.

"Wait a second," Leslie said. "Can you connect the laptop to your TV?"

"I don't know," Janie answered.

Javy flipped the laptop onto its side, checking the inputs, then jumped up and checked behind the tv. "Can I borrow the HDMI cable from your cable box?"

"Sure."

A few moments later, the TV came to life displaying the laptop screen. Javy scrolled through the menus to the flash drive window and moused over the video.

"Here we go. This picks up right where the last videos left off, with us going into the house."

The video opened with a wide shot of Mark and Cain standing on the front step. They nodded at each other, then Mark turned the knob. The door swung open quietly, the hinges giving none of the protest they might have expected from a vacant house. The camera moved in quickly and followed them inside.

The foyer was well lit. Sunshine flooded through the large bay window facing the front lawn. The house was immaculate —hardwood floors shined from a recent waxing, modern furniture sat sensibly placed around the room, and oil paintings of nature scenes dotted the walls. The men crossed the room and entered a living area featuring a huge sectional sofa, an oversized armchair, and a massive flat screen television.

"This is not at all what I expected," Mark said, turning slowly as he took in the surroundings.

Cain frowned. "Nor I, though my confusion is not from the look of the house. It's the energy. It's not what I expected."

"How so?"

Cain turned to look at the camera, then back to Mark. "I don't feel anything."

Mark eyed him thoughtfully. "Interesting."

"Let's not debunk the place in two minutes, guys," Javy said from behind the camera. "Let's see the rest of the house."

The camera followed them as they wandered through the estate. Each room was as extravagant and well-kept as the one before it. Apart from the foyer and living area, the ground floor featured a beautiful dining room, an amply stocked kitchen, a billiard room, full bathroom, mudroom, and various closets and pantries. Two separate staircases led to the upper floor, one off the living room, and another off a hallway near the mud room. The second floor was home to four bedrooms, all spacious and beautifully arranged, two more full bathrooms, a library, and an elegant spiral staircase leading up to the third floor attic.

As they toured the estate, Cain appeared to grow more anxious and frustrated with each room they discovered. While inspecting one of the upstairs bedrooms, Mark finally noticed his partner's discontent.

"What's bothering you, Cain?"

"I don't understand. There's nothing here. I know you don't take me seriously when I say spirits talk to me all the time, but it's true." Cain paused and scanned the room. "I can't hear them here. Not even a whisper."

"Maybe you need more time to find the energy?" Javy suggested. Though he was off camera, it was apparent in his voice Javy was worried about Cain giving up too soon. The show would be a waste if the paranormal expert called it not haunted on day one.

Mark seemed to sense Javy's feelings and patted Cain on the shoulder. "Don't get frustrated yet. I suspect this place has a lot to teach us. We're here for a reason, right? This place has a history. Derek Chamberlain himself said he had experiences here. Let's get settled in and see what's what."

Cain nodded, though he was clearly perturbed.

"Speaking of Derek Chamberlain," Javy said, "let's go check out this file he said he left for us. I'm excited to hear some first-hand accounts. Let's see what we're dealing with."

"Great idea," Mark said. "First, let's get our bags inside and pick bedrooms. I got dibs on this one. I could use a bathroom break and a few minutes to clean up as well."

"Sounds good," Javy answered. "Let's meet up in the living room in twenty minutes."

The camera left the room and drifted down the hallway to the library. Javy passed sturdy shelves packed floor to ceiling with books to the large oak desk dominating the center of the room. A manilla file folder with the name Chamberlain printed neatly across the front sat alone on top. The camera turned to face Javy, who smiled brightly.

"Stay tuned! It's almost story time!"

8

"So is this a slow burn story, or what?" Jared asked, giving Javy a scrutinizing stare. "Seems to me if our friend needs help, maybe we shouldn't be wasting time watching him pick out a bedroom?"

"I agree," Leslie said. "Can't we skip to what we need to see?"

Javy shook his head vigorously. "You need to see everything. You have to understand."

Before Leslie or Jared could argue, Janie cut in. "Let's not waste time arguing about it and watch the damn videos."

All three of them turned to look at her, stunned by the outburst.

"Okay," Leslie said, "no more discussion. We just watch."

Javy nodded and resumed the video. Mark and Cain sat on the large couch in the living room. The camera sat on a table, and Javy was visible on the edge of the screen, sitting in the armchair. Mark held the file folder in his hands, slapping it casually on his thigh.

"Alright," Javy began, "we are here at the Chamberlain

Estate. Our investigators have taken a few minutes to get settled, and we are about to dig into the notes Mr. Chamberlain left for us, documenting things he and other family members experienced in the house. Mark, would you do the honors?"

"Of course," Mark answered. He coughed and cleared his throat. "Here we go."

"First and foremost, I would like to welcome you to my home. I've asked you here to shed light on events that have troubled me throughout my life. As a young child, my siblings and I were told stories of strange occurrences in our family estate. These were not traditional ghost stories—no voices in the night, no apparitions floating through the halls. I would not call this house haunted. Rather, this house is a crossroads between this plane and the next. Originally, I intended to use this letter to relay some stories of my childhood. I have since decided not to do that. I worry my stories might influence your investigation by suggestion. I think it best you discover the intricacies of this place on your own, naturally. I will only say that much of what you see is not as it seems to be, and the things you can't see are legion. The doors are the key. I wish you great success and anxiously await your findings."

"That's it?" Javy asked.

"Yeah, that's all there is."

"Strange," Cain remarked. "That is not at all what I expected."

"Agreed. This doesn't give any stories at all. More like riddles," Mark said.

"Though it lacked any actual descriptions of activity in the house, it offers several interesting clues," Cain said.

"Such as?" Mark asked, raising an eyebrow.

Cain stood and paced slowly around the room. "He more or less claims the house is not haunted in any traditional sense, specifically noting no history of apparitions or disembodied voices. That could explain why I've had no success in communing with the spirits since we've arrived."

"Does that mean there are no spirits here?"

"Not necessarily. The world of spirits is vast and ever changing. It's entirely possible a form of spiritual energy exists here that I am not familiar with. I will need to meditate and reach out. If the spirits are here, they will come to me."

"You mean like a seance?"

"If you like. A thousand horror movies have twisted that term. Don't expect me to become possessed and speak Latin with the voice of an old woman," Cain said with a sly smile.

"Damn!" Mark joked. "So, do we wait until nightfall? I know you said the movies have twisted it, but I've never heard of a seance in the middle of the day."

"That part is true to an extent. I have always felt a stronger connection to the spirits at night, though I don't understand why. I suggest we gather after dark, perhaps ten or eleven, and I will attempt to reach the spirits. Until then, I'd very much like the opportunity to familiarize myself with the house. Wander around and see if I pick up any trace energy."

"I'd like to do the same," Mark replied. "I have a few gadgets I'd like to play with. See what kind of magnetic readings I pick up around here."

Cain nodded. "It would be worth ruling out any man-made or earthly phenomenon early on, so we don't waste time."

Mark gave an approving nod back to Cain. "Awesome. I was worried my experiments would offend you."

"Not at all. I do not disregard the effects of outside influence. I just know spirits exist alongside them."

"Sounds like we have a plan," Javy announced. "I have more gear to unpack, so since we'll go our separate ways for a while, I'm going to hook you guys up with cameras in case something noteworthy happens when you're alone. I don't want to miss anything, so please keep them with you and ready to roll. You don't have to record everything, of course, but be ready and if you think you might have something interesting, err on the side of caution and record it. Sound good?"

"Absolutely," Mark said.

"Very well," Cain replied.

"Okay," Javy said. "Let's go solo!"

9

The video paused, then returned to find the three men seated in the living area again, the flickering glow of the fireplace the only light in the room. Night had fallen and darkness pressed against the large bay window.

Leslie paused the video. "Where's the solo footage?"

"I could only take my camera with me when I left. All the solo footage is still at the house."

"The police searched the house, and they didn't find anything left from your visit," Leslie countered.

Javy nodded and grimaced. "Keep watching and you'll understand why."

"I'm sick of this wait and see riddle bullshit," Jared said.

"Please, just watch," Javy replied quietly, his eyes glued to the floor.

Jared prepared to fire back, but Janie leaned forward and pressed play. Jared locked eyes with her for a moment, then resigned himself to watching. He crossed his arms and flashed an angry glance at Javy, who now turned his attention to the screen.

"Okay, we're back together again. I'll review the footage later, but do either of you have anything of note to discuss from your solo adventures this afternoon?"

"I got nothing," Mark said. "No unusual magnetic readings. No strange angles or dimensions to any rooms. Nothing that would traditionally create an illusion of paranormal occurrences. How bout you, Cain?"

Cain held the silence for a moment as he considered his words. "This is—a strange place."

"How so?"

"I continue to find quite the opposite of what I expected. All places have whispers from the other side, even if only a little. This house is like a void. I haven't picked up the slightest hint of any energy here. That emptiness is like a vacuum pulling in different directions all at once. I've never experienced anything like it."

"Do you expect to have any success communicating tonight? Considering up to this point, you haven't felt any presence?"

"I honestly don't know. I'm eager to find out."

"Then let's begin," Javy announced.

"What do we need to do?" Mark asked. "Do we hold hands? Light candles? I'm a first-timer."

Cain smiled. "None of that will be necessary. Again, you let horror movies sway your perception. I need quiet, and I ask that both of you try to clear your minds and open yourself to the spirits."

"So, kind of like meditating?"

"Similar, yes."

The room fell into silence, and Cain dropped his head back on his shoulders to face the ceiling. The crackling hiss of wood burning in the fireplace became white noise against the quiet of the house. Minutes passed, then finally Cain dropped his head forward and stared at the two men.

"Did you get something?" Mark asked.

Cain's brow creased. "I don't know. The spirits didn't speak to me, but I feel something." He stood and looked around the room. "Follow me."

Javy jumped up and grabbed the camera from the stand, then fell in behind Mark as he followed Cain out of the living room and through the kitchen. They crossed the darkened room and entered the back hallway off the mudroom.

"It's here, but I can't see it," Cain said. He walked slowly down the hall, pressing his hands flat against the wall, sometimes holding an ear to the wood. "What is this?"

Mark ran his palm across the wall, then knocked in random places, attempting to find a hollow spot, but each knock sounded the same. He turned to Cain, who stared back in blatant confusion.

"I don't understand."

"Are you okay?" Mark reached out and put a hand on Cain's shoulder. "You don't look good. I mean, you look pale. Like, more than before."

Cain turned and stared at Mark, his eyes wide and unblinking.

"Cain? You with me?"

Cain held the frozen stare for another moment, then his shoulders slumped, and he let out a long exhale. He reached up and squeezed Mark's hand, still resting on his shoulder. "I'm okay. I think I need to lie down, though." He turned to face Javy and the camera, then looked back to Mark. "What the fuck is happening here?"

Mark flinched. It was the first time he'd heard Cain use profanity or fall out of the structured, proper speech patterns he always used.

"Sure, man. Let's get you to your room. It's been a long day for all of us. I think it's a good idea to wrap it up for tonight, get some sleep, and start fresh tomorrow," Mark said. He turned to the camera. "Sound good?"

"Yeah, of course," Javy replied. "I call it a successful first day. We end the night on a note of mystery." The camera spun to face him and he smiled in the darkness. "Catch you on the flip side, folks!"

IO

When the video resumed, the scene was still dark. The camera bounced erratically before focusing on Mark. He wore only a pair of blue gym shorts, and his hair was wild from sleep.

"Do you hear it?" Mark asked.

"Yeah, I hear it," Javy replied. "For the viewers, it's a little after two in the morning, and noises from somewhere in the house woke us up. We're going to investigate after we wake up Cain. Let's go."

The camera followed Mark into the hallway. He stopped outside Cain's room to find the door open and the bed empty.

"He's not here," Mark said.

"Damn, I hope he took his camera with him."

"Weird he didn't wake us up to go with him."

"Yeah, but maybe he was excited to have some action. Let's go find him."

They followed the noises, now a dull thumping sound, down the stairs. The living room and foyer were empty.

"Should we call out to him?" Javy asked.

"I don't know. In movies, when you do that, the noise stops. Don't want to mess up his gig."

"Good call," Javy replied. "Keep moving."

They crossed through the kitchen towards the back hall. The thumping sound increased in volume, but maintained a steady, rhythmic cadence. As they walked closer to the hall entrance, a new sound joined in with thumping—a frantic scratching sound.

Mark turned the corner into the hallway and stopped still. Javy nearly bumped into his back with the camera.

"What the fuck?" Mark said. He turned and stared wide eyed at Javy.

"What is it?" Javy whispered, scrambling around Mark to get the hallway into the camera's view.

Cain squatted near the end of the hall, facing the wall he had stopped at earlier. He rocked slowly back and forth, each forward swing bringing his forehead into the wall with a hollow thump. In contrast to the slow and steady rhythm of his upper body, his hands clawed at the wall, scratching wildly at the wood.

Mark walked slowly towards him. "Cain? What are you doing, big guy?"

When he got within a few feet of him, he gasped audibly.

"Oh my God," Mark whispered.

Javy hustled in beside him.

Blood smeared the wall. Cain's fingers were mangled, his nails broken and torn away, revealing the tender red flesh below. Blood seeped from the wounds, coating the wall and dripping in spurts onto the floor.

"Holy shit! What do we do?" Javy asked. "Is he sleep-walking?"

Mark put a hand gently on Cain's shoulder. "Cain, it's me,

Mark. You need to stop this. You're hurting yourself. Can you hear me, Cain? Let me help."

He put his arm around Cain's waist and gently pulled him away from the wall. From his crouched position, he rocked easily backwards and into Mark. Cain reached out for the wall, scratching at the air. He continued rocking his head back and forth, though the wall was now out of reach. After a moment of not contacting the wall, he whimpered.

"The door is on the other side. I have to open it," Cain whispered. At once, he stopped moving and turned to face Mark. "You can't see it, but I can. The door is here."

"Okay, buddy. We'll help you find the door. But let's get you fixed up, okay? Looks like you messed up your hands pretty good."

Cain stared curiously at Mark. Then he looked down at his fingers. "Oh," he said flatly. Seeing the bloody digits seemed to snap him out of whatever state he was in. He scrambled upright and leaned against the opposite wall of the hallway, looking frantically from the Mark to Javy and back again. "What happened? How did I get here?"

"We'll explain later. Let's go clean you up," Mark said.

"There's a first aid kit in my bag," Javy said. "Get him in the kitchen and I'll go grab it."

"Come on, buddy," Mark said. He put his arm around Cain and guided him back down the hall to the kitchen.

Javy flipped the wall switch, and a blinding flood of fluorescent light filled the camera. He sat the camera down on the large island and ran off screen to fetch the first aid kit. Mark led Cain to the sink and directed him to run cold water over his hands.

Cain hissed in pain as water splashed over the raw flesh. He turned to Mark, and his eyes brimmed with tears.

"Something is very wrong here."

"Spirits?" Mark asked. There was no trace of humor in his voice.

"No, I don't think so. This is something else."

"What else could it be?"

"I don't know," Cain answered. He turned back to the sink and watched trails of pink water and blood swirl down the drain. "I don't know what it is, but it scares the hell out of me."

II

"Okay, that was fucked up," Jared said, breaking the silence filling Janie's living room as the group processed the scene in the hallway.

Leslie paused the video and turned to Javy. "This is all legit? No special effects? Not some ruse between you and Cain to trick Mark?"

"It happened just like you saw."

Leslie held his gaze for a moment, then turned back to the laptop and resumed the video.

On screen, the trio of men gathered back in the living room. The golden haze of dawn flooded the bay window with amber light. Javy stepped around the camera and sat on the couch. All three men looked tired. Both Mark and Javy held mugs of coffee. They flashed looks of concern between each other and Cain, who sat on the other end of the couch staring at the bandages on his hands. Small drops of blood soaked through the wrap.

After a moment of awkward silence and soft slurps of coffee, Javy spoke up.

"How are you feeling, Cain?"

Cain's face twitched as he considered a response. "Aside from my hands, I feel okay, I suppose. Just confused."

"I really think you need to go to a hospital and get your hands looked at," Mark said, staring at Cain with concern. "Those open wounds can get infected. You ought to be on antibiotics just in case."

"We're kind of in the middle of nowhere here," Javy said softly. "It's a long ride to the nearest hospital. Between that and the wait to get in and out, we'd probably lose the whole day."

"Are you serious right now?" Mark asked as he spun his head toward Javy. "Cain's hands are an infection waiting to happen and you're worried about losing a day at the house?"

"No, that's not what I meant. If he needs to go, we'll go. No question. The safety of all of us is way more important than filming."

Mark stared at Javy, doubt lingering on his face.

"Do you want to go, Cain?" Javy asked. "Say the words, and we'll load up and get you checked out. We'll get back to investigating tonight or tomorrow. No big deal at all."

Cain continued to stare at his hands laying in his lap. "I'll be fine. I don't want to leave now. Not when things are happening."

"Are you sure?" Mark asked. He was clearly not comfortable with Cain's decision.

"Yeah, I'm sure. I'll be fine."

"Okay," Javy said. "If you change your mind at any point, let us know and we'll go. I mean it."

Cain nodded.

Javy looked to Mark for his approval. The two men stared at each other for a moment, before Mark threw up in his hands in defeat.

"Can you tell us what you remember?" Javy asked.

"It's strange. I don't remember much of anything. After we went to bed, I tossed and turned a bit, then dozed off. I have vague memories of dreaming of a door, and then the next thing I remember was waking up in the hallway with you holding me."

"You don't remember getting out of bed and going downstairs?"

"Not at all."

"Do you have a history of sleepwalking?"

"Nothing significant. I had a few episodes as a child, but nothing more recent."

"You talked about a door," Javy said, "right before you came to."

"Yes," Mark agreed. "You said something about a door being on the other side. You said we couldn't see it, but you could."

Cain stared at the two men in confusion. "This makes no sense at all. Nothing like this has ever happened to me."

"I was recording," Javy said. "I uploaded the footage to my laptop earlier. Would you like to see it?"

Cain turned his eyes back to his hands for a moment, then nodded. "I think I have to."

Javy stood and crossed the room, out of sight of the camera. He returned carrying a laptop and sat down next to Cain. Mark stood and walked around the back of the couch, positioning himself behind the two men so he could see the screen. Javy opened the file and queued the scene.

They watched in silence as the camera moved downstairs and through the main floor to the back hallway. As the camera focused on Cain bumping his head and clawing at the wall, Cain gasped.

"I don't believe this," Cain said.

He watched silently as the rest of the video played out, ending with him and Mark in the kitchen. Javy closed the laptop and returned to the chair. Mark wandered over to the fireplace and paced back and forth.

"Listen," Cain said. "I know I come across a little intense, but you guys know I wouldn't fake this, right?" He held up his bandaged hands. "I wouldn't do this to prove a point. You know that, right?"

"Of course," Mark answered. "Nobody is thinking that."

"No, not at all," Javy agreed.

Cain looked nervously back and forth between the two, then nodded and slumped back into the couch.

"So, what do we do now?" Mark asked.

"Well, I think we have to keep going. As long as you're comfortable, Cain." Javy said.

Cain considered for a moment. "There's something going on here I've never seen before. I don't know if it's spirits or something else, but I'm in this for the long haul." He held up his hands again and grimaced. "I'm not walking away without finding out why this happened."

"Same," Mark said. "I don't know what's going on here, but I'm ready to find out."

"Good," Javy said. "Let's get breakfast and regroup." He stood, crossed the room, and stopped the recording.

"You should have left."

The rest of the group turned to see Janie, her eyes fixed on Javy with a fierce intensity.

"Whatever happens next shouldn't have happened. You should have left."

"We didn't know. We couldn't have known what was going to happen."

"This is your fault. You took them there. You saw what was happening, and you kept going to make your goddamn show."

She rose from the couch and stepped toward Javy. Tears of rage, frustration, and grief trailed down her cheeks. "You did this."

"I'm sorry," Javy said. "If I could take it all back, I would, but I can't. They didn't want to leave either. It's not like I forced them to stay. We didn't know."

Leslie stood and put her arm around Janie, halting her before she got any closer to Javy. She'd never known Janie to be a violent person, but stress can make people do crazy things. "Okay, Janie," she said. "It will not help us find Mark if we fight. We need to finish the videos and see what happened. We need to find out how we can get Mark back. Right?"

Janie kept her eyes locked on Javy, her jaws clenched tight. Without a word, she let Leslie lead her back to the couch.

"How much more is there?" Jared asked.

"Not a lot. Things went downhill pretty quickly after that. We were only there one more night."

"One more night? This was three months ago. Where the fuck have you been since then?" Leslie asked.

Javy closed his eyes, and a shiver passed through him. "Just watch the videos."

12

The video resumed to find the trio back in the hallway behind the kitchen. The deep scratches from the previous night's events were highly visible in the light of afternoon. Brown smears and splatters of dried blood on the wall and floor further proved the vicious enthusiasm Cain had shown during his search for a door that did not exist.

Again, Mark rapped his knuckles against the wall, searching for any sign of a recess behind, but each knock rang solid. Cain stood at the end of the hall near the back staircase, observing.

"You won't find anything," Cain said flatly.

"Sure doesn't seem like it," Mark replied.

"There's something else, though."

"What's that?"

"Since this morning, since what happened last night, I've started picking up energy waves. It's strong in this hallway, especially at that spot, but it's not the only one."

"You feel energy coming from other places in the house?"

"Yes. Whatever this is, there's more than one."

"What do you think it is?"

Cain paused as he considered his words. "I honestly don't know. It's not any kind of spirit energy I've ever felt before. That hasn't changed. It's very strong though—too strong."

"Where else do you feel it?" Mark asked.

"There are at least two upstairs. I can't be certain, though. It flows and surges at strange intervals. No kind of pattern I can identify. The more I walk around, I keep feeling them in new places where I felt nothing before. It makes no sense, but I think they are moving around. This one here in the hallway seems to be consistent, but the others come and go."

"I understand you don't know what exactly you're feeling," Javy said, "but do you have any theories? Either of you?"

"I don't know enough to formulate a theory," Mark answered. "The things Cain is describing don't jibe with any natural phenomenon I know of. My goal was to bring a scientific view of the spiritual findings Cain brought us. I wasn't prepared for our experiences to be unusual for him."

"Neither was I," Cain said. "You see it in all the ghost hunting shows. When they say a haunting isn't spirits, they automatically jump to demons. I don't believe in demonic activity. I've seen no evidence of it. That said, this is definitely not spiritual in any sense I have ever experienced."

"So what's the plan?" Mark asked. "If it's not spirits, then I don't guess it will do us any good to communicate."

"I think we stay the course. When we arrived, I felt nothing at all, but things have revealed themselves the longer we stay. I suspect that will continue. I don't know if we will have much luck before the sun sets. Whatever is happening here seems to share that in common with the spirits. It seems more active after dark."

"I think now would be a good time to do some video journal entries. I would like to document how each of us is feeling as we progress through the investigation," Javy said. "Not that any of us are keeping secrets, but I'd like to present us all the opportunity to speak freely without concern for any judgement or opinion from the rest of us. I'll set up the camera in the library upstairs and we can each take turns recording a quick update. You guys up for it?"

"Sure," Mark said.

Cain nodded, but remained silent.

"Cool," Javy said. "I'll get it set up and go first. I'll call you up when I'm done."

The video stopped, then resumed with Javy sitting at the large desk in the library.

"So it's day two in the Chamberlain Estate. Though nothing at all like I expected, I think it's safe to say our investigation has been a success already. What happened last night with Cain was wild. I admit, for a while there, I was worried about his mental state. I didn't know if he was going to want to continue, but I'm relieved to see he seems to be shaking it off pretty well. Mark is a sponge, taking everything in. I think he may be a little disappointed he hasn't been able to demystify anything yet. My gut tells me there will be more opportunities. I think we're at the tip of the iceberg here and I can't wait to see what else we can discover."

Javy reached forward and stopped the video. When it resumed, Mark had taken his place behind the desk.

"Hello internet world! Mark Landon here. Our first night at Chamberlain proved to be pretty strange. I don't know what happened there. I truly don't believe Cain is messing with us. I also considered the possibility Cain and Javy are in on this together, and maybe how I react to things is the real investigation here. From a realist point of view, both things are possible. But I follow my gut, and my gut says Cain and Javy are both on the level. In that case, I really don't know what's going on here.

The damage to Cain's hands is real. I know that. I still think he needs to see a doctor, and honestly, I'm a little pissed Javy didn't back me up on that. He says our safety is a priority over this project, but he was quick to move along as soon as Cain said he didn't want to go. Hopefully, he'll be okay. Hopefully, I can find answers. That's what I'm here for. That's all I've got for now."

The video stopped, then resumed once more. Cain sat with his arms draped on the desk in front of him, staring at his bandaged hands. For nearly a full minute, he sat motionless. At last, he raised his head and looked into the camera.

"I feel I've expressed my opinion thoroughly to the group at this point. There is only one thing I would add that I have not said to Mark and Javy. The spirits have guided me through my life, steering my decisions and warning me of danger. Since I cannot hear the spirits here, I feel exposed. I can't be sure that we are safe here."

He lifted a hand and stared at the dried blood spots on the bandage.

"In fact, I don't think we're safe at all."

13

For the first time since they started the viewing, Javy moved from his position leaning against the wall, crossed the living room and paused the video.

"Before we go any further, please believe me when I say that what you are about to see is real. I swear to you I didn't mess with anything."

They all looked at him as he glanced anxiously from person to person, waiting for a response. Janie spoke for all of them by clicking play on the video.

The video resumed and night had fallen once more. The camera sat on the coffee table in the living room, and Javy crossed in front of the lens. He sank into the overstuffed chair and pulled his knees up to his chest.

"Hello again," he said. "Unfortunately, it has been an uneventful day. After the events of last night, it feels pretty underwhelming. But, we had no action until late last night, so maybe things will get moving again tonight. Cain excused himself to bed a while ago. He seems to be pretty worn out. Mark is staying close by him in case he sleepwalks again. I have decided not to risk missing anything, so I've got the camera batteries fully charged, and I plan to stay up on watch until sunrise. The days have been quiet, so I think it'll be okay to sleep through the morning. I've got a book to read, a pot of coffee to drink, and seven hours to go. Now we wait."

Javy stood and reached for the camera, but before he pressed the button to stop recording, a loud thump shook the ceiling above him.

"Javy!" Mark's shout echoed down the staircase. "Get up here!"

"Oh shit," Javy said. The camera jostled wildly as he snatched it from the table and ran to the staircase. "Guess we're done waiting."

When the upstairs hallway came into view, Mark was on the ground, his back against the wall. Cain moved quickly down the far end of the hallway, around the corner, and out of sight.

"What happened?" Javy asked. He gripped Mark's hand and helped pull him to his feet.

"I heard him get up and start walking around, so I came over here to check on him. I opened the door, and he blasted into me. Knocked me down. He looked like he did last night, like he was in a trance."

"C'mon," Javy said. "He's heading for the back stairs. Back to that hallway is my guess."

Mark jogged down the darkened hallway past the bedrooms and turned the corner to the back stairwell. The camera bounced after him. Mark hit the top of the landing, but Javy slowed to a stop, turning the camera towards the wall.

"Uh, Mark?"

"What?" Mark asked, anxiously wanting to get downstairs.

"Was this door here before?"

The question caught Mark off guard, and he walked back to Javy.

"Definitely not."

A black iron door with intricate carvings filled the wall near the stairwell.

"I think we would have noticed this," Javy said.

"This isn't possible," Mark said. For the first time, a quiver of fear accented his voice. "No fucking way." He reached for the large iron ring that served as a handle, but Javy knocked his hand away.

"Don't touch it. I don't think we should open this."

Mark hesitated, then a screech of metal hinges floated up the stairs, piercing through the silence of the house.

"Cain," Mark said.

He turned and raced back to the staircase. Javy let the camera linger on the menacing black door for a second, then followed Mark. The staircase dumped them into the back hallway, where Mark stood motionless. Another door, identical to the one they found upstairs, stood open. The scratches were gone, but the bloodstains from the night before were visible on the floor in front of the opening. Cain was nowhere to be seen.

"Holy shit," Mark whispered.

They creeped down the hall, listening for any sign of Cain, stopping at the open door. A crude stone staircase disappeared into an inky darkness.

"He went down there, didn't he?" Javy said.

"He did," Mark agreed.

"We have to go down there, don't we?"

"We do."

"Fuck me."

"Cain," Mark called into the darkness. "Can you hear me?"

His voice echoing into the void was the only response.

"We need lights," Mark said.

"Hold on," Javy said. "I've got flashlights in my bag." He sat the camera down on the ground and sprinted down the hall, his footfalls fading until all was quiet again.

The camera bounced and turned. Mark's face filled the screen.

"I don't know what's about to happen, but I don't have a good feeling. Janie, I hope I'm being dramatic, but if something happens to me, I hope you know I love you. If we get out of this thing, I'm coming home tomorrow. If not, then I want you to know every minute I spent with you were the best minutes of my life, and I'm going to do everything I can to get back to you. Every fiber of my soul is telling me to walk away from this door and leave this place, but I can't do that. I can't leave Cain down there. You know I can't."

The sound of footsteps thumping through the house became audible again. Beams of light flashed into the hallway, and Javy appeared, carrying two flashlights.

"You ready?" Mark asked.

"No."

"Me either. Let's do this."

Mark handed the camera back to Javy, took a flashlight from him and descended the stairs. Javy blew out a deep breath and followed him into the dark.

14

Leslie pulled Janie into a fierce hug. Warm tears soaked her shoulder, and her own eyes burned. Javy and Jared both stared awkwardly at the floor while Leslie tried to comfort her.

"It's okay," Leslie whispered. "We're going to get him back. That's why we're doing this. We're gonna get him back."

Janie peeled herself from Leslie's grip and wiped her eyes. "Let's finish this."

Leslie handed her a box of tissues, plucked one for her own use, then resumed the video once more.

The camera followed Mark down the stone stairs. Even in the glow of flashlights, he was barely visible. The darkness was absolute, preventing the light from piercing more than a few feet. The staircase descended ten, twenty, thirty steps with no end in sight.

"Jesus, how far down does this go?" Javy asked. "It's some kind of basement, right? It can't be that deep."

"We're not in a basement. That door shouldn't have been here, and neither should this, whatever this is."

The stairs curved and walls narrowed until Mark was brushing against both sides with his shoulders as he continued down. Javy's breathing behind the camera increased, coming in rapid bursts.

"I'm claustrophobic, man. I don't think I can keep going," Javy wheezed between breaths.

"I see light," Mark called out behind him. "Not much, but some. I think we're close to the bottom. Keep moving and stay close. We're almost out."

The camera continued to move, focused downward at the back of Mark's legs. Slowly, the darkness lifted, and Mark stepped down onto a dirt floor. The walls opened up and Javy stepped to the side, gasping at the air.

"My God," Mark said.

Javy jerked the camera upright and scanned the area. They found themselves in a cavernous room with a large pool of black liquid glimmering in the center. A faint breeze drifted across them, and the air was dank and stale. The room pulsed with an ambient glow emanating from the pool. At the edge of the pool, Cain's towering figure stood, his back to them, transfixed by the shimmering lights.

"There he is," Mark said.

"Let's get him and get the fuck outta here," Javy said.

They walked cautiously across the cavern, careful not to startle him. Mark put up a hand to stop Javy, then moved a few paces to the left, allowing himself to come into Cain's peripheral vision at a small distance.

"Cain, it's me. Your buddy, Mark. We need to go back up the stairs, okay?"

Cain turned his head and looked at Mark. "I found the door."

"I know you did," Mark said in a quivering voice. "Right

where you said it would be. Me and Javy found another door. Upstairs. You want to go see it?"

"All doors lead to the end."

"To the end of what?"

"Everything."

"Is that where we are? The end of everything?"

"See for yourself," Cain said. He held out his hand for Mark to grasp.

Mark took his hand gently, minding the bandages, and tugged softly away from the pool, but Cain did not budge.

"See for yourself," he repeated. His hand clamped on Mark's, fresh blood erupting through the bandages. He took three long strides into the pool, dragging Mark into the black liquid with him. Mark thrashed against the water, trying to plant his feet and pull away, but Cain held Mark's hand in an iron grip.

"No!" Javy shouted as both men disappeared under the surface. The liquid surged against the bank from the disturbance. The camera dropped from Javy's hands and smacked into the soft dirt beside him. He ran to the edge of the pool, stopping short of stepping into the liquid.

"Mark! Cain! Fuck!"

The waves settled, and the pool resumed its odd shimmering. Neither man returned to the surface.

"Please," Javy screamed. A thousand echoes mocked him from every direction. "Come back." He dropped to his knees and broke into tears. "Please, come back."

The water swelled again, and Javy jerked his head to the pool. Twenty feet out, two heads emerged. Mark and Cain rose out of the water and trudged to the bank.

"Oh, thank God. You came back." Javy said. He scrambled to his feet and ran to the camera, picking it up out of the mud. "Now let's get the fuck out of here."

He spun the camera back to the men and screamed. Mark and Cain stared back at him with black eyes, swirling with the same flecks of light on the surface of the pool. He spun and raced away from them, back to the staircase. The camera bounced erratically as he raced up the stairs, panting and gasping in fear and exertion. When he reached the top, he let out a bellowing sob.

A solid stone wall marked the top of the staircase.

The door was gone.

15

The group all turned in unison and stared at Javy. His lip quivered as he watched himself on screen slapping at the stone wall, screaming in absolute terror. For the first time, the realization Javy was a victim in all of this, and not a reckless bystander who started the chain of events, hit home.

Leslie chewed her lip as she considered what to say, regretting the hostile attitude she had been giving him. She turned to Jared, who looked equally uncomfortable with the sudden change of perspective. He returned her glance, then lowered his eyes to the floor. Only Janie could keep eye contact as Javy struggled to compose himself.

"I'm sorry this happened to you," she said.

Javy sniffed and cleared his throat, battling tears. "So, this part of the video goes on for a while. Obviously, I've spliced all these together for you guys to watch. I cut out a lot of this because nothing happens. Just more of what you see now."

"How did you get out?" Jared asked, the accusatory tone in his voice no longer present.

"Eventually, I fell asleep. Maybe I passed out. I don't know. I was so afraid." His voice cracked with emotion and he paused for a moment. "I was afraid they would come up after me."

"Did they?" Leslie asked.

"No. Play the rest of it."

Leslie nodded and resumed the video for a final time.

Javy's face filled the screen. He sat on the top step, his back to the wall, rocking back and forth. Dirt and grime streaked his face, held in place by dried tears.

"Battery's almost dead," he croaked, his voice hoarse from screaming. "Don't think we're getting out of here. They're still down there, I guess. I hear things, but I don't know anything anymore. I'm sorry we came here. If anyone ever sees this, I want you to know I take the blame. We never should have come here."

He fell into silence and closed his eyes. The video skipped an edit, then Javy reappeared. His eyes were wide open and soft crunching sound filled the speakers. He turned to the wall and gasped. Scrambling to his feet, he grabbed the camera and pointed it at the wall. The stone surface had vanished, replaced once again by the black iron door. Javy placed a shaking hand on the door and pushed. The door swung out into the hall with a screech.

"Holy shit," he whispered.

The camera bounced out into the hallway, then turned back to the darkened staircase.

"Mark! Cain! Can you hear me?" Javy screamed down the staircase, wincing at the ragged pain in his throat. "Please!"

He waited a moment for any sound of a voice or movement below, but the silence held firm.

"I'll come back for you guys," Javy shouted. "The door is open! Come up if you can. I'll get help, and I'll come back!"

He turned and stepped into the hall. Bright sunlight filled

the lens, causing the video to auto adjust. Javy jogged down the hall and into the kitchen. The camera came to an abrupt stop as he entered the living room. Derek Chamberlain sat in the overstuffed chair with one leg crossed, dark sunglasses covering his eyes.

"Mr. Romero. It's nice to see you again. It's been a while." He motioned to the couch. "Please, have a seat."

"Mr. Chamberlain, we need help. There's a door, and they're down there, and something happened to them, and—"

"Calm down," Derek said. He rose from the chair, crossed the room, and put a comforting arm around Javy's shoulder, guiding him to the couch. "Tell me what happened. I'm anxious to hear of your experience."

Derek took the camera from Javy and sat it on the table facing Javy, then sat down beside him. "You mentioned a door. Start there. What door?"

"In the back hallway. It wasn't there before, but then it was there, just like Cain said. I thought he was crazy, but it was really there."

"Was it a black door? Made of iron?" Derek asked.

Javy's eyes lit up. "Yes! You've seen it before?"

"Of course. That's why I brought you here."

Javy's relief dissipated quickly. "Mark and Cain. They're down there."

"*Down* there, you say, so this door revealed a staircase down?"

"Yes," Javy answered, blinking in confusion. "I thought you said you'd seen it before. Wouldn't you know that?"

"There are many doors here that go to many places. Sometimes up, sometimes down, sometimes straight ahead. What was at the bottom?"

"A pool. A black pool."

"Wonderful," Derek exclaimed. "And Mark and Cain, they went into the pool, didn't they?"

"Yes."

"But not you, Javy."

"No," Javy said, his voice quivering in fear and confusion. "How do you know that?"

Derek leaned in toward Javy, close enough to whisper in his ear, then slid his sunglasses down the bridge of his nose. Javy screamed and scrambled away from Derek, flipping backwards over the back of the couch. Derek was not facing the camera, but his head turned enough for Janie and the rest of the viewing party to see the glistening black shine in his eye.

Javy popped up behind the couch, continuing to backpedal away from Derek. He bumped into the wall behind him and pressed himself against it as if he could disappear into the wood.

"You said you wanted to investigate the beyond, didn't you?" Derek asked. He slid the sunglasses back up over his eyes. "I delivered. It's more than you could imagine. Infinitely more." He waved his hand at the empty seat beside him. "Please sit. I have a proposition for you, Mr. Romero."

16

"I fucking knew something was off about this guy," Leslie said. Her face flushed red. "He lied to the police."

Javy turned and looked at her blankly. "This is the last video. When it's over, we decide what you want to do." He turned, walked out of the living room, and seated himself at the kitchen table, his back to the group.

Leslie started to speak, but Janie silenced her with a quick wave, then she played the last video. Leslie let out a sharp exhale through her nose in frustration, then returned her attention to the screen. Jared bounced his eyes back and forth from the video to Javy in the kitchen.

On screen, Javy had slowly approached the couch and sat down, albeit as far from Derek as he could. He sat hunched forward, legs tight, ready to run.

"When my family built this house all those years ago, it wasn't by chance. It drew my grandfather to this spot. There's power here. The rumors about us are true. Dabblings with the occult? Sure. It's as good a name for it as anything, I suppose.

For decades and generations, my family has worked to uncover the secrets of the universe. The answers were here. We just had to find them." He paused and a smile spread across his face. "And after all this time, I did."

"What did you do?" Javy asked.

"I got the doors to open. The doors have been a fixture here the whole time, shifting from one area to the next. No pattern or rhythm to it. But none of us could ever get them open. After my parents died, leaving me here alone, I was resigned to following my ancestors down the same path of disappointment. Close to the truth, yet unable to obtain it. And then, just like that, one day the door was open. Perhaps I was chosen. Perhaps it was mere coincidence. What is two hundred years to the infinite? A blink? A fleeting thought? I found the door open at last and a staircase leading deep underground. At the bottom was the pool. I could feel it calling me in. I still feel it. And, oh, the things I saw."

Javy stared in horror as Derek smiled, lunacy ravaging his normally handsome face.

"I stayed there for some time, though time is of no importance. When I emerged from the pool, so full of knowledge, I discovered time had carried on quickly. I entered the pool in December 1988. I emerged to a world far advanced, thirty years later."

"Thirty years?" Javy said. "That's not possible."

"Isn't it? You yourself were only down there a short time, and yet months have passed."

"What?"

"It has been nearly three months since you and your companions crossed the threshold."

"That's bullshit. It's been maybe a few hours," Javy cried, nearing hysterics.

"To you, yes, probably so. But time is of no importance."

Javy stood from the couch and drifted to the edge of the camera's view. "I have to get help. I have to go."

"Yes, you do. In fact, that's why I brought you here. This world, this *existence,* is fleeting. The key to eternity lies behind these doors, and we will build a new kingdom upon it. You and your friends were the first, but you won't be the last. In fact, it's a blessing in disguise that you did not enter the pool. I expected to find you all exposed to the truth, and I would have to recruit more to join our legion. Your resistance has created more opportunity. Your friends, they have loved ones, yes? People who care about them. Bring them here."

Javy froze, staring in disbelief. "I don't understand."

"Maybe not," Derek said. "But once you enter the pool, you will. You will understand so much. Now go. Take your camera. Show them what you've seen. They will come. How could they not? Who can resist eternity?"

Derek stepped to the camera, lifted it from the table, and carried it across the room. Javy's pale face and bloodshot eyes bounced on the screen.

"I will be waiting—and watching."

The video stopped, and the screen went dark.

PART THREE

I

Before Janie or Leslie could react, Jared was out of his seat and charging toward the kitchen at Javy. Javy lurched from the chair and turned in time for Jared to slam into him, knocking him back onto the counter. Jared grabbed a fistful of Javy's hoodie and pulled him forward until the men were nose to nose.

"What the fuck was that? You working with this Chamberlain guy? Trying to trick us into coming with you to that house?" Jared shouted, his face a mask of rage.

Javy stared blankly back at Jared's snarling face, as if he knew this outburst was coming.

"Talk, motherfucker!"

Leslie entered the kitchen and put a hand on Jared's shoulder. "Easy," she whispered.

"Fuck that. This guy is out to get us."

Leslie ignored Jared and turned her attention to Javy. "Can you explain this?"

"It's the only way," Javy answered quietly.

"The only way to what? Get us killed, too?" Jared said.

"For fuck's sake, Jared," Leslie hissed. "Shut up."

"He's not dead," came a soft voice from behind them.

Leslie and Jared both turned to see Janie standing in the doorway with tears in her eyes.

"He's not dead," Janie repeated. "You said 'get us killed, too,' but he's not dead."

"I know he's not," Leslie replied.

"I know how this looks," Javy said, bringing everyone's attention back to him. "It looks bad, but I swear I didn't come here to make you guys part of that sick bastard's cult. I don't know if Mark and Cain can be saved or not, but I knew I couldn't do it alone. I need help. Cain was a loner. He never told me about any family or friends close to him. Mark has you guys, and he needs you. I need you."

Leslie studied his face while he spoke. She held his gaze for a moment, then slapped Jared's arm gently. "Let him go."

"Nope,"

"God dammit, Jared. Let him go!"

Jared saw the fury in her eyes and sighed. He released his grip on Javy's shirt and stepped away.

"So you're saying your plan is to double cross Chamberlain, and maybe all of us together can save Mark?" Leslie asked.

"And Cain," Javy answered.

Janie bolted past them and disappeared around the corner into the front hall. They heard the closet door pulled open and rustling from within. She returned with her jacket in her hands.

"Let's go."

"This is ridiculous," Jared said. "Listen to yourselves. We need to call the cops right now and hold this guy until they get here. I don't know what that shit was on those videos, but I'm not about to run off and play hero to rescue your brother from some kind of ghost cult."

"Then stay here," Leslie said coldly. "We're going. It's four hours to the house from here. We can be there by midnight if we're lucky."

"How do you know that?" Jared asked.

"Because I fucking went there, you asshole. While you've had your head up an Xbox's asshole, I've been trying to find my brother!"

Jared winced at the fierceness in her voice. "Babe, I didn't mean it like that."

"You never do. I love you, Jared, but if you're going to stand in my way on this, then you can get the fuck out."

He froze at her words, realizing how close he stood to the edge.

"We don't have time for this," Janie said from the hall. Her eyes no longer showed any sign of tears, but now featured a resolute intensity. "We have to go."

Jared sighed and shook his head. "Fine, let's go."

Leslie gave him an icy stare, then nodded. "You ready?" she asked, turning to Javy.

"I'm scared to death, but I'm ready."

"Me too," Leslie replied. "Let's do it."

Janie turned immediately and was out the front door. Leslie let Javy go in front of her and followed him through the kitchen. Jared reached out and grabbed Leslie's hand as she passed, pulling her gently.

"I'm sorry, babe. I lost my cool."

Leslie tried to give him another blast of cold stare, but softened. "It's okay," she said. She leaned up and kissed him quickly. "Come on."

He nodded and followed her out of the house, locking the door behind him. He bumped into Leslie, who had stopped on the step. Janie and Javy stood on the sidewalk, staring at the black Lexus idling in the road in front of the house. The driver's side window rolled down, revealing Derek Chamberlain, still wearing his sunglasses.

"You've done well, Mr. Romero," he called out. "I look forward to welcoming you all into my home. I trust you know the way?"

Sensing another outburst from Jared, Leslie put a hand back against his chest. "We know the way," she called back.

"Excellent. I will see you soon."

Without another word, he pulled away from the house. The four of them watched as his tail lights dimmed, then disappeared as he turned the corner.

"Mother fucker," Jared whispered.

Silently, they got in Leslie's car, backed out of the driveway, and pulled away.

Janie turned and watched the house fade from view through the back windshield, wondering if she would ever see it again.

2

The car was ominously quiet as Leslie steered them through what seemed to be an endless onslaught of cornfields. Harvest time was around the corner, so the corn stalks were high and thick. Leslie kept a tight grip on the steering wheel, staying focused on the very real possibility of a deer emerging from a field and prancing into her front end.

They had stopped to fill up the gas tank at the station down the street. Leslie didn't mind. The thought of following Derek Chamberlain's sleek Lexus to an uncertain confrontation made her even more unsettled than she already was. Jared had gone inside the station, then emerged carrying an arm full of bottled water and Gatorade for the road, while Leslie worked the pump.

After an hour of brooding silence, Jared spoke tentatively.

"I'm not sure exactly what the plan is when we get there," he started, "but I think we had better come up with one."

"This was your idea, Javy," Leslie said. "What do you think?"

"I don't know. I was only there for two days—well, at least for me it was two days." He shuddered. "Let's hope the door is there, and that it will open."

"It will," Janie said, barely audible over the hum of the tires.

Javy and Jared both turned to look at her. Leslie watched her face in the rearview mirror.

"This is all happening for a reason. The door will be there, and it will open."

"Okay," Jared said. "Let's roll with that. What about Chamberlain? I expect he'll be there waiting when we arrive. What are we going to do about him?"

Leslie sighed. "I don't know, Jared. I'm with you. We need a plan. But given how things currently stand, I think it's probably a waste of time. We don't know what's going to happen, so we have to be ready for anything."

"She's right," Javy said.

The car fell silent again, miles passing in a blur of fields and farmhouses. Leslie felt like she was driving on a treadmill with stock photo scenery playing on a loop.

Eventually, the rural landscape transitioned into more urban locales as they neared the outskirts of Cincinnati. The sky glowed from the distant city lights, but shortly after they appeared, they faded as they entered the last leg of the trip back into the countryside northwest of the city. Leslie asked Jared to pull up the map on his phone and gave him the Chamberlain Estate address from memory. The robotic voice droned out driving directions, and the bottom of the screen reported forty-five minutes until arrival.

"We're getting close," Javy said. With every passing mile, he had grown more fidgety, squirming in his seat.

Leslie cast intermittent glances at him in the rearview

mirror. Her focus had been on finding Mark and on whatever waited for them at the house. Now, she sympathized with the anxiety and genuine fear Javy felt to be going back after what happened. The visual of him slapping at the stone wall where the door had stood only minutes before flashed in her mind. His willingness to return to save Mark despite his dread touched her.

"I don't think any of us have said it yet, but thank you for doing this," Leslie said. "After everything you went through, I can't imagine what it must be like to go back. You're doing a good thing, and we'll do everything in our power to keep you safe. We're going to get Mark and Cain, and all of us are getting out."

Javy remained silent in the back seat, but his eyes glittered with tears. Janie reached across the seat and squeezed his hand. He turned to look at her, then gently squeezed her hand in return. A single tear broke free and trailed down his cheek. He wiped it away and turned his eyes back to the window.

They finished the rest of the trip in a silence interrupted only by the navigation system giving directions. Just before midnight, the robotic voice announced their destination was on the right. Leslie slowed as the front gate appeared in her headlights. She turned into the driveway, following the curving path through the trees. The house was ominous, a pale glow from the front window the only light to break up the darkness. She followed the split in the driveway and pulled up behind the black Lexus. She shut off the engine and exhaled deeply. A shadow moved into the window, revealing Derek Chamberlain awaiting them inside.

"Be ready for anything," Leslie said.

No one else spoke, and Janie was the first to open her door. The others followed suit and gathered in a huddle in front of the house. The shadow of Derek Chamberlain disappeared from the window, and a moment later, the front door opened.

"Welcome to my home," Derek said. "Won't you come inside?"

3

Janie led the way into the house, giving a stony stare to Derek as she passed him. She felt woozy as the now familiar house became a reality around her. Seeing it on video had not done it justice. The ceilings were high, making the room feel larger than it was. The fireplace crackled and cast twisting shadows on the walls.

Jared and Leslie followed her into the living room, with Javy sticking closely behind them. Derek closed the front door, and the sound of the deadbolt snapping into place echoed throughout the room. Leslie jerked her head at the noise but didn't speak.

Derek crossed the room and sat in the chair near the fire. "Please, have a seat," he said, motioning toward the couch.

"Where is Mark," Janie said.

Derek smiled at her. "You'll see him soon enough, I'm sure."

"No, I want to see him now," Janie said.

Before Derek could reply, Janie turned and marched out of the living room and into the dining room. She heard the scramble of footsteps behind her, but paid them no mind. She followed the path, now ingrained in her mind, from multiple viewings of Javy's videos through the kitchen and into the hallway branching off the mudroom.

"Janie, wait," Leslie called.

Janie blocked out her voice and hurried down the hallway, stopping at the blank section of wall where the door had been. She saw the faint brown stains near the baseboard, remnants of Cain's bleeding hands, but the door was gone. She felt the rest of the group gather around her.

"I told you," Javy whispered. "The door might not be here."

"The other door," Janie replied. "The one you and Mark saw upstairs." She continued down the hall to the backstair case. The others followed her up the stairs and found another solid wall.

"Fuck," Leslie hissed.

"Maybe Derek knows how to make the doors appear," Javy suggested, his voice quivering as he spoke.

"I don't think we have any other choice," Jared said. "If Chamberlain can make this happen faster, then we need him to do it. The quicker we're out of here, the better."

"Fine," Janie said.

She led them through the upstairs hallway, though the determination in her stride was gone. They descended the stairs back into the foyer. Derek still sat in the chair, an amused expression on his face.

"No doors?" He asked. "It's frustrating, isn't it? I know the feeling well."

"Can you make one appear?" Leslie asked.

"Please, sit down. All of you."

"Answer the question, pal," Jared said.

"I will answer your questions when you sit down," Derek replied.

Again, Janie took the lead and lowered herself onto the couch. Leslie and Javy followed and sat beside her. Jared resisted for a moment, staring defiantly at Derek. The two men held each other's gaze. The corner of Derek's mouth twitched upward into the hint of a smile, furthering Jared's hostility.

"Just sit, Jared," Leslie said.

Jared bit down, clenching his jaw, but stayed silent and sat down on the end of the couch next to Javy.

"Thank you," Derek said with exaggerated relief. "There's no need to be so tense. You are all on the doorstep of infinite knowledge. You should be excited. I'm no fool. I'm sure you've come here tonight with the sole intention of *rescuing* your friends. You probably think I'm a madman." He chuckled as he spoke. "Had I not grown up here, I would probably think the same thing. No, my friends, I am not a fool or madman. When the time comes, you will see for yourselves. You will see more than you could have ever imagined. Mark and Cain do not need rescuing. In fact, they need nothing at all. You will join them, and together we will usher in the true reality."

"We need the door to appear," Leslie said. She kept her tone cordial, masking any trace of hostility. "Can you make one appear?"

"Oh, if only I had that power," Derek said. "We are but pawns in the scheme of eternity. We have no power here, save for the power of knowledge. No, the doors appear only when *they* want them to."

"They?" asked Leslie.

Derek smiled. "You will know them soon enough. Unfortunately, until such time that they see fit to let you in, we have no choice but to wait. You'll find ample accommodations for you all upstairs."

"Bullshit," Jared exclaimed. "We're not staying here."

"If you want to *rescue* your friends," Derek said, "then you have no choice. They are beyond the doors. You won't find them until a door appears and opens. None of us can make that happen, but it will happen. Oh yes. Until then, we will wait."

"It's fine," Janie said. "We'll wait until they let us in."

"Smart girl," Derek said.

"Let's go," Leslie said. She stood and motioned for Jared and the others to follow suit. "I think we could all use some time to collect ourselves."

They gathered at the foot of the stairs. Janie turned back to Derek, still seated by the fire.

"Where will you be?"

"I will be around. Fear not, I wouldn't miss this for the world."

4

Leslie stood by the bedroom door as the rest of them filed into the room, then locked the door behind them. She recognized this room as the one Mark had chosen upon their arrival. Of course, there was no trace of him or his belongings—she knew as much from the police investigation of the house—but yet she felt his presence. She didn't believe in ghosts or spirits, but the knowledge that he had been here a few short months ago gave the room a lingering aura.

"I don't like this at all," Jared said.

"I don't either," Leslie agreed, "but we don't have a choice."

"It won't be long," Javy said. He had placed himself in the corner, staring out the window at the trees cloaking the sprawling front lawn. "You saw how fast it happened to us. It only took two nights for doors to appear. I think it will happen sooner now."

"How do you know that?" Janie asked.

"I don't know. I just feel it." He turned from the window and looked at Janie. "Don't you?"

Janie nodded in silent reply, then sat down on the edge of the bed.

"I know this will sound like a bad idea, but I think things will happen faster if we don't stay in one room together."

"Fuck yeah, things will happen faster," Jared shouted. "That psycho downstairs will pick us off one by one."

"Stop," Leslie said. "You've heard and seen everything I have. Something crazy is happening here, but it's way more than Derek Chamberlain murdering people. I think Javy is right. At the very least, we should break into pairs. Jared and I will go stay in the room across the hall. Janie, are you okay with Javy staying with you?"

"Yes."

Leslie turned her gaze across the room. "Javy?"

"That's fine. Like I said, I don't think we will wait long."

Leslie nodded. "It's settled then." She grabbed Jared's hand and led him toward the door. "If anything happens, you stay together and come get us immediately. No wandering off on your own. We go together. Are we all clear on that?"

"Yeah," Javy answered. He stared back at all of them with a grim expression. "I just hope it's enough. You all saw the videos. You saw how Cain was. Like he wasn't in control of his own body." He paused and sucked in a deep breath. "Be ready for anything, okay?"

"Absolutely," Leslie said.

She unlocked the door and led Jared into the hallway. Javy watched them enter the room across the hall, then closed the door. He turned to find Janie had crawled up near the headboard of the bed. She clutched a pillow tightly against her chest.

"They don't understand," Janie whispered.

Javy shook his head. "You feel it, don't you?"

Janie nodded. "I feel him. He's here."

"I'm sorry this happened."

Janie watched Javy cross the room and sink onto the bed across from her. His red-rimmed eyes glistened with emotion. The youthful enthusiasm he portrayed in the early videos was lost. Now, his pale face reflected fear and grief and guilt.

"Do you think we can bring them back?" Javy asked. "You saw their eyes on the video. Whatever happened to them when they went into the pool, do you think it can be undone?"

"I don't know." Janie let one hand go from the pillow she clutched against her and reached across the bed. She took Javy's hand into her own and squeezed it gently. "I know that if there's anything left of the real Mark, he will fight. If there's a way to come back, he'll find it."

"I hope you're right," Javy said. He squeezed her hand in return, then stood and crossed the room. An armchair sat near a table in the corner, and he dragged it to the window and sat, knees pulled into his chest, his head laid back. "I think things are going to happen before morning. I don't know what, but we should rest. Whatever happens, we'll need all the strength we can get."

Without a reply, Janie rolled over on the bed. She adjusted her grip on the pillow, pulling it tightly against her chest and burying her face in the soft fabric. She fancied she could smell a faint trace of Mark in the pillow, and she let that be a small comfort. Her eyes closed, and she drifted to sleep.

5

Leslie paced around the room while Jared watched from the bed. He sat with his back pressed against the headboard and his legs crossed in front of him. Back and forth, she walked from one end of the room to the other.

"Would you sit down and take a breath?"

"I can't," she said, never breaking stride. "I don't like this—having no control."

"I know. I can't believe I'm saying this, but we have to ride it out and see what happens. Twenty-four hours ago, I would have called bullshit on us being here and doing what we're doing, but here we are. I don't like it any more than you do, but I don't think we can make anything happen. We have to wait for it."

She stopped and turned to him, ran a hand through her hair, then sighed. "You're right. I know it. I'm just having a hard time accepting it."

"What, that I'm right about something?" he asked, grinning.

She smirked at him in return, but her posture softened and

she climbed onto the bed beside him. He held out his arm, and she snuggled up against him. He held her with one arm and twirled her hair with his other hand.

"I'm sorry for being such a hardass about all this today," he said.

"I know," she answered. "I'm glad you came with us. I was kind of bluffing when I threatened to leave you at Janie's."

Jared chuckled. "I wouldn't have let you go without me."

They sat in silence for a few minutes, listening to the wind blow. A nearby tree branch scratched softly against the window. Beyond that, the house was silent around them.

"This is fucked up," Jared said.

"I know."

"I really don't like knowing Chamberlain is down there somewhere. Part of me is screaming on the inside to call the police and be done with this. This isn't real life, what's happening right now. It can't be."

"I know what you mean, but after what we saw in the videos, I don't know what to believe anymore."

"It could all be fake, you know?"

"Why would anybody do that?" Leslie asked. "Fake something like this? What would be the point?"

"People are fucked up. They do stupid shit for no reason all the time."

"No," Leslie said, "not like this. Trust me, all this supernatural shit goes against everything I believe. But, after what we saw, I know something is going on here. I know Mark is close. I feel it."

Jared fell silent. She was right. As much as he wanted this to be an elaborate hoax, there was more to it than that. He was the last person to buy into ghosts or spirits or whatever the hell this thing was, but this place was different.

"You think they're okay over there?" Leslie asked.

"You worried Javy might try something?"

"No," she said, "I trust him. They're just fragile. If something happens tonight, I hope it happens to us first. I'm worried about what Janie will do if she thinks she can get to Mark. I'm afraid she'll run off without us. Based on the videos, that is not a good thing to do here."

"Javy knows better than any of us what this place can do. I think he'll stay on point and get us if anything happens."

"I hope so."

"So, do we just go to sleep then, I guess?"

Leslie laughed at the thought. "Sure, let's take a little nap while we wait for the mystical infinity doors to open up and lure us into their cult."

Jared chuckled and kissed Leslie on top of her head.

"I love you, babe," he said. "Let's make sure we all get out of here, okay?"

Leslie leaned up and kissed him, letting her lips linger on his for a moment. "I love you, too. And yes, together is the only way we leave."

"Agreed."

6

Janie opened her eyes and knew right away she was dreaming. The bedroom where she'd fallen asleep was gone. She stood in a rolling field. Tall grass swayed gently back and forth on a delicate breeze. The sky was a strange swirl of purple and black clouds blocking out the sun, yet she could see well enough. She gazed at the foreign landscape. It was mysterious, but instead of feeling uneasy, she was overcome with a sense of comfort like she had not felt since the days before Mark left.

Mark.

His name rolled off her tongue. Her voice sounded strange in this dreamscape, and the grass seemed to lean away from her when she spoke, as if the interrupted silence disturbed it. A crash of thunder erupted above her and she flinched. She looked to the sky; dark clouds swirled with an increased intensity. The air was alive with energy and goosebumps broke out all over her body. She suddenly felt vulnerable, but there was nowhere to hide. She spun around, looking for any place where she might find shelter. The land behind her rose moderately to a crest, blocking the view of what lay beyond. Thunder crashed again, jolting her into action, and she ran up the slope. When she reached the crest, she froze.

A man sat on the ground with his back to her. His knees were pulled up to his chest, and he cradled them in his arms. She couldn't see his face, but she didn't have to. She knew the shape of his back, the muscular tone of his arms. Those same arms had been wrapped around her so many times.

"I found you," she whispered.

"I knew you would."

His voice sent chills up her spine. This was further proof that she was dreaming. If she was awake and this was real, she would've run to him and threw herself into his arms. Her dream-self showed restraint.

"Where are we?" she asked.

"Here."

"Where is here?"

"Everywhere... and nowhere."

Janie walked the few feet between them and sat next to him on the grass. She reached over and wrapped her hand in his.

"I've missed you so much. My life was empty without you."

"This life is nothing."

"What do you mean?" Janie turned to look at him, but he kept his eyes on the sky in front of them.

"I've seen what we are. Simple and insignificant. The trivial things that were everything before—it all means nothing. I've seen the truth now. That's why I left, remember? To find the truth. It's more than I could even fathom."

A cold certainty filled Janie's thoughts. "You can't come back, can you?" Her heart broke as she said the words, because she already knew the answer. "Whatever happened to you when you went into that pool, it can't be undone, can it?"

"The truth cannot be unseen."

She squeezed his hand and fell quiet. They sat in silence with the occasional crash of thunder. Lightning flashes lit portions of the sky. The longer she watched, she saw giant faces swirling in and out of the violet clouds.

"Would you like to see?" Mark asked. "I can show you."

"Does it mean we can stay together?"

"If that's what you want."

"It's all I've ever wanted. What do I have to do?"

Mark slowly turned to look at her. His eyes were empty black voids.

"Wake up, Janie. Wake up and find the door."

The sky erupted with a deafening roar, and the world disappeared in a blinding white flash. A blast of wind forced her backwards, and she sank into the soft ground. The surface shifted beneath her, and then she was falling through darkness. She closed her eyes and waited for the end.

When she dared to open her eyes, she found herself back on the bed. Javy was curled up in the chair by the window, snoring softly. She climbed slowly out of the bed, careful not to make any noise, and tiptoed across the room, opened the door, and slipped out into the hallway. She stood still in the hallway and listened for any sounds coming from Leslie and Jared's room, but heard nothing.

She felt guilty, but she had to go. Mark had shown her where the door was. She saw it swirling in his inky black eyes.

7

Derek Chamberlain sat by the fire. His eyes were closed, but he did not sleep. He was listening. The hissing and pops from the fire became white noise, and he strained his ears. His guests had been quiet for some time. Any footsteps from above would certainly grab his attention, but they were not his focus. He was listening for a door. It was a subtle sound, imperceptible to most, but over the years he had learned to identify the sound—to feel the vibration of one plane of existence colliding with another.

He smiled as he pondered the wonders of the vastness beyond the doors. To be free of the confines of human existence was breathtaking. To know everything was to be God. His guests would know the feeling soon, as Javy's little documentary crew now knew. He longed to speak with them. Initially, he had been disappointed to find Javy did not go into the pool. However, he stifled his disappointment and seized the opportunity to use Mr. Romero to recruit more people to join his cause. They would join him in infinite knowledge, and they would be his soldiers. He would stand above all men and create a new existence. The door opened for him after generations of failure. Surely, he was chosen to be a god among men.

Two separate sounds occurred simultaneously, and pulled him from his notions. He perked up in his chair. Above him came the soft sounds of footsteps. He heard the faintest of squeaks from a door hinge. One of his guests was on the move. Likely one of the women, based on the lightness of the tread.

More enticing than the sounds from above was the ever-so subtle change in vibration on the ground floor. It was a feeling he cherished more than any other. A door had appeared.

He sat erect, debating his next move. Should he seek the door and satisfy his urge to dip back into the pool and perhaps meet his new companions, or should he allow his guest to find it first? It was no coincidence one of them left their room within seconds of a door appearing. Reluctantly, he eased back into the chair and waited. As much as he desired to revisit the void, he thought it best to let things happen naturally. If the door wanted one of his guests to find it, he should not intervene.

As he allowed himself to relax and listen, a figure emerged from the foyer. Derek flinched, having heard no one approaching. A towering frame filled the doorway, dark hair hanging limply in front of its face. Derek's initial fear melted away.

"Cain, my brother. I have longed to speak with you, now that you have seen the truth." Derek stood and motioned toward the couch. "Please, won't you sit with me? We have such incredible things to discuss, yes?"

Cain stood motionless in the doorway. Flickers of light swirled in his otherwise black eyes.

"Are you still in shock?" Derek asked? "It is quite a lot to take in, especially if you weren't expecting it."

"You betray yourself," Cain said. "Claiming this gift of infinite wisdom as a power to rule. You know everything and yet nothing."

Derek considered Cain's words. A sliver of uncertainty pierced his mind. "I'm afraid I don't understand?"

"That is correct," Cain replied. "You've been told the secrets of the spirits, but you twist their words to suit your intention."

"Spirits? You must know now there are no spirits. You've seen the void. Ghosts and poltergeists are figments of imagination. Yes, there are beings in the void, but Cain, my friend, they are not spirits."

"They are spirits in their purest form. Again, you cannot see the truth despite claiming to know all. You subvert their message and seek to wield that power to your own gain." Cain took a step into the room toward Derek. "The spirits will not allow that."

For the first time, Derek felt a tinge of fear. "Please," he said, making no effort to hide the desperation in his voice. "Let us go together into the void, and I will show you."

Cain took another step, and Derek stepped back.

"The spirits know and see all. The hearts and minds of men are open to them, and they have seen all they need to see of yours."

Cain leapt across the room at impossible speed. Derek turned to run, but he did not expect the attack and moved too late. Cain's large hand locked around Derek's throat. He lifted him into the air, then slammed his body into the ground. Derek's head bounced violently off the hardwood floor. He grabbed and clawed at Cain's hands, but the big man's grip was like iron, and Derek felt his esophagus collapsing.

Cain pushed Derek by the throat until his head rested on the bricks of the fireplace. Derek stared helplessly up at him, the firelight dancing with the swirling white flickers in his black eyes.

"You have dishonored the gift bestowed on you by the spirits. The spirits have judged you unfit and appoint me executioner."

Derek's face was blue, and his own black eyes were fading to a milky white interlaced with red trails of bursting blood vessels. Cain lifted Derek by this throat once more and slammed his head into the fire. Sparks and embers erupted in the fireplace, showering onto the floor. Cain held firm and the leaping flames first ignited Derek's hair. Derek wheezed what would have been a scream through his crushed vocal cords. His face blistered and bubbled, then charred black. Cain's own hand did the same, but he did not react. He held firm and watched the last of the Chamberlains cease to be.

8

Leslie jerked herself upright in bed to a thundering thump below them. Jared stirred beside her and sat up.

"What the fuck was that?" he asked.

Another thump rattled the walls, and Leslie scrambled to her feet and ran into the hallway. Just as Jared emerged from the bedroom behind her, Javy opened the door to the room across the hall. Leslie peered behind him but saw no one.

"Where's Janie?" she asked, panic filling her voice.

"I don't know. That bang woke me up, and she was gone."

"Fuck!" Leslie shouted.

The sound of a male voice and shuffling floated up the stairs.

"That bastard Chamberlain's got her," Jared said, and he pushed past Leslie and raced down the hallway.

Leslie followed him, with Javy bringing up the rear. They tore down the stairs and stumbled into the living room. Leslie didn't know exactly what she expected to find, but the scene before her was not it.

A giant of a man she recognized immediately as Cain held Derek Chamberlain's head in the fire. The stench of burning flesh filled the room, and Leslie fought the urge to vomit. Derek lay still, clearly dead, but Cain still held him in the flames.

"Holy shit," Javy whispered, then gagged.

The sound caught Cain's attention, and he finally released his grip on Derek's throat. He turned and stood to face the group gathered in the entryway. Jared stepped in front of Leslie defensively, but Cain did not make any move to advance on them.

"Cain," Javy said.

"You got what you wanted," Cain said. "You wanted to find the unknown, and now you have."

"This isn't what I wanted," Javy said, his voice cracking with emotion. "I'm sorry this happened."

"It is as it was meant to be. The spirits have always called to me, and now they have shown me their true form."

"Why did you do that?" Jared asked, pointing at the lifeless corpse still burning in the fire.

"He was not worthy of the gift bestowed upon him."

"Where is Janie?" Leslie asked. The shock of the scene before them had relented enough for her to remember Janie was missing.

Cain tilted his head as if he were thinking. Leslie got the feeling he was looking up, but his black eyes gave no sign.

"She has been called to the void."

"Is that where Mark is?" she asked.

"Yes."

"Where is the door?" Javy asked. "We have to stop her."

"It is too late. She is with Mark. They are together."

"That's right, and we're going to get them out of here together. And you." Leslie said.

"I will return to the void, and that is where I will stay. I have no reason to stay on this plane any longer. The spirits call me home."

Cain turned from them and walked away into the kitchen.

"Follow him," Leslie said with bitter determination.

They moved after him, careful not to get too close. Leslie didn't feel threatened by him, despite the savage violence he was capable of. They trailed him at a safe distance as he turned down the back hall. Leslie expected to see the iron door where it had been in the video, but the wall was undisturbed. Cain continued past it and up the staircase at the end of the hall.

They reached the second floor landing, and again Leslie was disappointed to see the walls undisturbed. This was where Mark and Javy found a door in the video. She wondered if Cain was misleading them, but when they rounded the branch in the hallway, the door stood open only ten feet past the bedrooms they had fled moments earlier. Leslie cursed herself for not noticing, but the noises from downstairs had distracted them. Cain disappeared into the darkness, and the group gathered at the open door.

"This is it," Leslie said. "This is what we came for."

"Do you really think Mark can come back from this?" Jared asked. "Can he go back to how he was?"

"I don't know," Leslie said. It rang hollow in her mind, because she thought she knew, but saying it out loud would crush her. "We have to try."

"Yeah," Javy agreed. He stared into the darkness with terror in his eyes, but he held his ground. "I brought these guys here. I'm not leaving them if there's any chance we can help."

"Alright," Jared said. "Let's do this." He stepped in front, took Leslie's hand, and led the way down into the dark.

Javy took a deep breath, said a silent prayer, and followed.

9

When Janie reached the bottom of the stone staircase, she knew what she would find. It was exactly the same as it had been in the video—a vast cavern with a large pool of inky black liquid. Like in her dream, Mark sat on the ground near the edge of the water, his arms wrapped around his knees. She crossed the cavern and sat next to him.

"I found you, again."

"I knew you would."

"This time it's real, isn't it?"

"Yes. As real as this world can be."

"My world wasn't real without you."

"Do you want to see what it really is?" Mark turned and looked at her.

"Do you think I should?"

"You wouldn't be here if they didn't want you to see, but ultimately, it is your choice."

She considered his words, but there was no doubt in her mind. "I want to see."

Mark nodded and stood. He reached out and Janie took his hand. They took slow steps into the water. She expected it to be cold, but the liquid was warm and soothing against her skin. The hairs on her arms stood up, and she felt her body ripple with an energy unlike anything she had felt before.

"Should I hold my breath?" she asked.

"No."

She nodded and stepped further into the pool. The darkness swelled up around her thighs and then their hands, still laced together, submerged. They took two more steps, and the liquid lapped her chin. She stopped for a moment, and she squeezed his hand.

"I love you," she said.

"I love you, too," he replied.

And then she dipped under the surface.

Despite his words, she held her breath. When her lungs burned, she finally exhaled, fighting a wave of panic that proved to be unnecessary. She breathed easily, no different from before. The floor fell away, and she floated. She realized she was closing her eyes and cautiously opened them. At first, she saw nothing but the occasional spark of white swirling in the darkness. Then, as her eyes adjusted, she made out colossal forms around her. Some were humanoid, others like giant creatures beyond anything she could imagine. There was no noise, aside from a dull hum that vibrated her body. She looked at Mark. He floated beside her, a look of absolute peace and clarity on his face. It reminded her of the look he had when they would hold each other after making love. To have him with her again, no matter where it was, filled her with happiness and she smiled in the dark.

As if he sensed her feelings, Mark turned and smiled back. For an instant, his eyes flashed back to the sparkling blue she knew so well, and she knew she was home. Wherever this was, it was home.

Mark held out his arm and pointed below them. In the distance, a pale green light pulsed. They drifted down together, closer to the light. She noticed they moved freely through the void, with no effort required. Her body moved toward wherever she focused. She suspected if she closed her eyes, she would stop moving indefinitely. With Mark's hand in hers, floating in this nothingness with him at her side was all she wanted, but Mark seemed intent on showing her the source of the light.

As they approached, Janie saw the pulsing light emanated from an orb the size of a grapefruit. The humming vibration intensified the closer they got until it reached a constant buzz surging through her body like electricity. The orb flashed rhythmically within an arm's reach away.

Mark pointed to the orb and nodded. Janie tightened her grip on his hand, then cautiously placed her free palm on the orb. Her senses erupted—touch, taste, smell, and sound merged into a hybrid of undulating energy. Her being scattered in infinite directions, surging through endless threads of a cosmic tapestry. In an instant, she knew everything that had ever been. She saw the earth for what it truly was—a grain of sand on an endless beach, insignificant and yet a living piece of an infinite whole. And watching over all of it were the colossal beings of the void. She knew them, just like they knew her. Cain called them spirits. Derek thought of them as gods. Mark considered them the truth. They were the source of everything.

Janie let go of the orb, and the swirling darkness returned. She turned to Mark, who stared at her with a satisfied smile on his face. She pulled him to her and they kissed while the eyes of eternity observed their love. After months of grief and torment, Janie found the peace she longed for.

She was home.

IO

Leslie, Jared, and Javy emerged into the cavern at the bottom of the stairs. Cain stood at the edge of the pool, waiting.

"You are welcome to enter the void if you wish, however, time is short."

"What do you mean?" Leslie asked. "And where is Janie?"

"She has gone to the void," Cain answered.

"Oh no," Javy moaned and dropped to his knees.

"I have to see her," Leslie said. Her eyes glistened with tears.

Cain nodded. "I will call for them." He turned back toward the dark pool, but did not speak.

After a moment, the surface of the water rippled, and two heads surfaced. Mark and Janie walked out of the pool, hand in hand, and stood beside Cain.

Leslie sobbed and ran toward them.

"Leslie, wait," Jared shouted.

She threw her arms around Mark and hugged him fiercely,

bawling into his shoulder. Mark put his free arm around her, but never let go of Janie's hand.

"Why is this happening?" Leslie whispered through her tears.

"It was meant to be," Mark replied. "Don't cry for me."

"We're home," Janie said.

Leslie turned to Janie, whose black eyes swirled with pinpricks of brilliant light, and pulled her into the hug. "You can't come back, can you?"

"No," Janie said, "but I wouldn't want to." She turned and smiled at Mark. "We are where we are supposed to be."

"What am I supposed to do? I don't want to leave you, but I'm afraid to go in there," Leslie said, her eyes shifting to the black pool behind them.

"If you don't want to see, then you are not meant to see," Mark said. "Go, sister, before it is too late."

"What do you mean by too late?" Jared asked. He had walked across the cavern and put a comforting hand on Leslie's back.

"The door will close soon," Cain said. "This place has served its purpose. When the door closes this time, it will not open again. Not here."

Leslie sniffed and wiped her cheeks with her shirtsleeve. "Will I ever see you guys again?"

"Yes," Janie and Mark answered in unison.

"All things are part of the whole," Mark said.

Cain turned and stepped into the pool. "The door will close soon. Unless you wish to join us, then you must go."

"C'mon, Leslie," Jared whispered. "We have to go."

"I love you guys," Leslie said. She wrapped Mark and Janie into a hug once more, then turned and ran toward the stairs.

Javy still sat on his knees, tears streaming down his face.

"Gotta move, man," Jared shouted as they ran past him.

"My fault," Javy said. "This is all my fault."

Jared stopped at the bottom of the stairs and groaned in frustration. "Go," he shouted to Leslie, then he turned and sprinted back to Javy. He grabbed him by the arm and yanked him to his feet. "Let's go!"

Javy relented and followed Jared to the stairs. They climbed, panting from exertion. At last, sunlight filled the tunnel and Jared saw Leslie waiting at the top of the stairs. They covered the remaining few dozen steps and collapsed into the hall. Leslie pushed the black iron door closed and fell into Jared's arms, sobbing hysterically. Javy watched as the door faded and disappeared, leaving a blank wall.

"Let's get out of here," Jared said.

They stood and trudged to the staircase and into the foyer. The smell of burning flesh had faded, but the body of Derek Chamberlain still lay with its head in the fireplace. The fire had burned out completely.

"Jesus," Leslie said, "how long were we down there?"

"Maybe ten minutes," Jared said.

"Not here," Javy said flatly. "Could've been days."

"What are we going to do about him?" Jared asked. "Just leave him? Nobody knows we're here."

As if in answer, a deep groan emanated from the walls of the house. All around them, the paint cracked and peeled, the floors sagged, and the windows faded, blocking out the sun.

"What the fuck?" Jared said. "Go!"

The three of them ran to the front door and into the driveway by Leslie's car. They turned back to the house and watched in disbelief as the foundation crumbled, the walls cracked and split, the entire structure aging in fast forward. Then, with a deafening crash, the house collapsed, sending a spray of dust and debris in all directions.

"Holy shit," Leslie said.

"I think we'd better go. I don't want to be here when the police show up."

"Yeah," Leslie agreed. There were no neighbors nearby, but that crash had to have been heard for miles. It was only a matter of time until authorities were notified.

Leslie got in the passenger side. She was in no shape to drive. Jared walked around to the driver's side and opened the door. "Let's go, Javy."

Javy stood staring at the wreckage of the Chamberlain estate, ignoring Jared.

"Fuck," Jared whispered. He walked back around the car and put a hand on Javy's shoulder. "We did the best we could, man."

"We never should have come here," Javy said. "This is all my fault."

Jared sighed. "I know it's tough, but you can't think like that." Jared paused and then the faint sound of sirens caught his attention. "You hear that?" Jared asked. "We have to go right now."

Javy bit down on his lip, then followed Jared to the car. Jared jumped into the driver's seat and started the engine. He whipped the car in reverse, careful not to go too fast and risk leaving skid marks, then drove as quick as he could handle through the tree-lined curving driveway. They pulled onto the road and turned right, away from town and the approaching police and fire trucks. He watched the rearview nervously, but the emergency vehicles were out of sight.

Javy watched out the back window as the remnants of the Chamberlain estate faded from view.

EPILOGUE

Javy Romero saw the name displayed on his ringing phone and picked it up in resignation. If he didn't answer, she would keep calling back. He dragged his finger across the screen, then tapped the speaker icon before sitting the phone back on the desk.

"Hey, Leslie."

"Hey. How are you?"

"Same as I was yesterday and the day before that," he answered.

"Yeah," Leslie said. An awkward moment of silence passed before she spoke again. "Have you decided what to do about the police?"

"No, not yet," Javy said, then sighed. Rejoining society after being a missing person for three months would not be a seamless process, especially when the truth about his disappearance was so unbelievable. He'd spent the last few weeks laying low at a friend's apartment. He knew he couldn't hide for the rest of his life, but he wasn't ready to face the inevitable questions and accusations from police.

"I worry about you."

"I know, but I told you, I'm fine."

"You're not fine, Javy. That's bullshit. None of us are fine."

Javy grimaced. Some form of this conversation had replayed between them multiple times, but Leslie never let up.

"Okay, we're not fine, but we're doing what we have to do to keep going."

Leslie sighed into the phone. "Look, I know you feel a massive amount of guilt for what happened, and I understand it. But, it's not your fault. You never could have known what would happen in that house. You had good intentions."

"Look what my good intentions got me."

"See," Leslie said, "you're doing it again. I lost my brother and my friend, but I don't blame you, and you have to stop blaming yourself."

Javy dropped his head. He knew she was right, but he could not let it go. It felt wrong to have a good day. Any waking moment he spent not thinking about the Chamberlain estate and Mark and Cain was time spent not taking responsibility for what happened.

"How's Jared?" Javy asked, trying to change the subject.

"He's Jared. Doesn't talk about it much, and does his thing, business as usual. I guess I need that, though. If I didn't have him dragging me along, I'd probably be just like you. And that's why I keep calling. I'm trying to help you move on. I don't want to leave you behind, dealing with this on your own. It's not your burden to carry."

"I appreciate you, Leslie. I do. I'm doing better, honestly."

"I want to get together soon. Jared and I can meet you half-way, and we can have dinner or something."

"Yeah," Javy said. "That would be nice."

"I'm still going to call you."

Javy chuckled. "Maybe we can skip to every other day?

Seriously, you don't need to call me every day. I'm okay." He did his best to keep his tone cheerful and light. "Give my best to Jared."

"I will. If you need anything, call me. Please."

"I will."

"Okay," Leslie said. "Take care and we'll talk soon."

"See ya," Javy answered, then ended the call.

He leaned back in the desk chair and gazed at the ceiling. Leslie's concern was appreciated, but the fact of the matter was he had to do something. He couldn't move on with life knowing Mark, Cain, and Janie were lost in some cosmic void.

He returned his attention back to the computer displays on the desk. A search engine with several open tabs filled one screen. They all featured variations of "mysterious iron door" or "phantom doors". The other screen had YouTube opened up and search results for the same. He scrolled through the video thumbnails, looking for anything that seemed legit. Most of it was clearly faked ghost videos or clickbait. For days, he had scoured the internet for anyone reporting something similar to what he experienced at the Chamberlain house. If it happened there, it could happen elsewhere. He needed to find a door.

As he scrolled through a seventh page of video results, one of them caught his eye, and he scrolled back up to it. His eyes widened. The still photo thumbnail featured a young woman standing next to a black iron door with a speech bubble over her head that said, "This wasn't here before?!?!?".

His heart rate soared as he leaned closer to the screen and examined the designs in the door. They were the same. He clicked the video and sat impatiently through an ad. The video started with the girl on the thumbnail standing in a lavishly decorated living room.

"Hey y'all, it's Sherry! I'm here with my best friend and camera girl Christy at my family's vacation house in Georgia.

Me and Christy came down for a little weekend getaway, but something weird is going on. I've been here a bunch of times since I was a little girl, so I know this house pretty well. When we got here today, I found this."

She pointed offscreen, and the camera turned to a wall across the room with a black iron door. She walked across the room and stood beside it.

"This door was not here before. You want to see something even more weird? Check this out."

She motioned for the camera to follow her as she walked the length of the wall and around the corner to reveal a large dining room.

"There's no door on this side of the wall. So, to recap, there's a mysterious door that wasn't here before that goes nowhere. And now, for the ultimate piece of 'What the Fuck Theater,' I called my dad to tell him. Had to go outside and find a signal because the service sucks here. He thought I was joking and asked me to send him a picture. I go back inside to snap the pic, and it's gone. No door. This all happened yesterday. Really creepy stuff. We almost didn't stay here, but we're adventurous girls, so we figure we'll see what happens. We get up today and the door is back. It's locked too. Won't budge. Not that it goes anywhere, obviously. So, I ask you, internet people. What kind of weird magic is happening?"

The video ended, and Javy scrolled quickly down to the comments. It was an even split between "That's scary" and "That's fake as hell". Surging with excitement, he searched through Sherry's channel info and found her social media links. He snatched up his phone and opened the Twitter app, then found her profile. Her DMs were open, and he frantically typed a message.

I watched your video about the door in your vacation house. I know what it is, and I'd like to come and investigate if you'll allow it.

He groaned and shook his head. This girl would never invite some random dude to her vacation house to investigate a mystery door. There had to be another way. He considered for a moment, then an idea sparked in his mind. He checked her YouTube channel subscriber count. She had a respectable following, and from the looks of her other videos, she was working to increase it. What if he could guarantee her more subscribers? It was a disgusting idea. He didn't want to endanger more people, but there was no other way. Referencing his channel was a huge risk. If she knew about the Chamberlain incident, she could blow the whistle on him, but his gut told him he may not get another chance. He deleted the text he had already typed and started over.

My name is Javy Romero, and I have an opportunity for you!

Acknowledgments

I truly didn't know if I could write this book. Up to this point, my longest story was around six thousand words. I wrote the first chapter over a year ago, prior to releasing my debut short story collection The Collapse of Ordinary. I knew this story had the potential to be something bigger than I'd ever written, but at the time I wasn't ready. After the release of the collection, I knew it was time to see if I could tell a longer story. I hope it worked.

I love this story, and it will always be special for two reasons. I proved to myself that I could write a full length book, and also that The Collapse of Ordinary was not a fluke, and I could do this again. Much like with that book, this one doesn't happen without the support of several people.

I would like to thank my wife Jessie for never wavering in her support. I wouldn't be able to do this if she didn't have my back. I love you very much, and like I said back in the beginning, this one's for you.

Thank you to my beta readers Brandon Applegate, Chuck Buda, Matt Wildasin, and Don Tackett. Your input was critical in keeping me from falling into plot holes.

Matt Wildasin knocked it out of the park again with the cover art. You were my first friend in the writing community, and I'm proud to be in the trenches with you.

Brandon Applegate fine tuned this story to what it is today.

His edits were invaluable. This book isn't the same without you.

Chuck Buda is the guy keeping me in line. Whenever I have questions, need advice, or just want to bullshit about Ancient Aliens, I know he's just a call or text away. I appreciate you more than you know.

And of course, my biggest appreciation goes to you beautiful people who took a chance and picked up this book. From the bottom of my heart, thank you. There are a million things you can do with your time, and you chose to spend some of it reading my story. That means the world to me, and I hope you enjoyed your stay!

About the Author

Steve L Clark is an author of horror and dark fiction from Southwest Ohio where he lives with his beautiful wife and three wonderful children. He is the author of the short story collection The Collapse of Ordinary as well as a contributing author to the anthology Dark Words: Stories of Urban Legends and Folklore edited by Matt Wildasin, both of which are available on Amazon.

Follow Steve on Twitter @SteveLC8349 for updates on future projects.

ALSO BY STEVE L CLARK

Short Story Collections

The Collapse of Ordinary

Anthologies

Dark Words: Stories of Urban Legends and Folklore

Edited by Matt Wildasin

www.ingramcontent.com/pod-product-compliance
Lightning Source LLC
Chambersburg PA
CBHW030145010826
48973CB00002B/741

* 9 7 8 1 9 6 5 3 1 6 0 0 9 *